Queen of Ice

Read more for young adults from Duckbill

Read more by Devika Rangachari

Queen of Ice

DEVIKA RANGACHARI

duckbill

For Amma and Appa—my reason for being, my reason to be

Duckbill Books
F2 Oyster Operaa,
35/36 Gangai Street Kalakshetra Colony,
Besant Nagar, Chennai 600090
www.duckbill.in
platypus@duckbill.in

First published by Duckbill Books 2015

Text copyright © Devika Rangachari 2015

Devika Rangachari asserts the moral right to be
identified as the author of this work.

10 9 8 7 6 5 4 3

ISBN 978–93–83331–18–5

Typeset by PrePSol Enterprises Pvt. Ltd.

Repro Knowledgecast Limited, Thane

Also available as an ebook

Children's reading levels vary widely. The general reading levels are indicated
by colour on the back cover. There are
three levels: younger readers, middle readers and young
adult readers. Within each level, the position of the dot
indicates the reading complexity. Books for young
adults may contain some slightly mature material.

SIGNS OF GREATNESS

DIDDA

I have heard the tale many times over—and yet, I feel a thrill course through my body at each narration. It is as if the words are breathing life into me, making me into a person of flesh and blood from a mere idea.

'It was dark,' my mother says, 'sometime between deepest night and early dawn. I was in pain, such pain that I thought I would die.'

'But you didn't,' I murmur as I snuggle closer to her, covering my toes with the hem of her voluminous silk skirts. The snow continues to fall outside, each layer covering the previous one as if it were a package waiting to be trussed up and loaded on to the back of a pack mule.

The fire roars in the chamber, meanwhile—a somewhat noisy intrusion into our time together.

'No, I didn't,' my mother agrees. 'Just when I thought I couldn't bear it any longer, just when I wanted to give up the fight, there you came in a rush.'

'And the midwife held me up and said, "Behold, your majesty, you have a girl!"' I chant, the familiar words slipping off my tongue so easily that I could have recited them in my sleep. How often had I heard this story? Ever since I could understand words and frame them into pictures in my mind, I suppose. But I had reached the hard part of the tale and a frown creased my brow.

My mother sighed and reached for my foot, tugging it out gently from under her skirts and caressing its deformed contours. I flinched as I always did when someone touched it. It didn't hurt—at least, not physically—but my mind filled with the usual anger and sadness.

'Why was I born like this?' I ask, as if I hadn't already asked this question a hundred times over.

'It is god's will,' replies my mother, as always. Her eyes are filled with tenderness but as I turn my face away to hide my tears, she cups my chin in her hands and shakes her head. 'No tears, my Didda,' she says firmly. 'You must try to accept your lameness, not fight it.' She wipes the tears that are coursing down my cheeks and makes me meet her eye. 'You are destined for greatness, my child. Haven't I always told you that?'

'How will I be great? And when?'

She smiles at the childish question. 'Some day. You have to be patient.'

I know what she means—the story that had done the rounds of the court soon after I was born and ensured, perhaps, that I wasn't stifled at birth for being a girl—and a deformed one at that. The astrologer, a fearsome, impossibly tall man, who held the court in thrall to his powers, had told my father that the signs proclaimed greatness for me.

And so, I was allowed to live. Yet I often saw my father look at my cousin, Vigraharaja, his late brother's son who lived with us, with longing in his eyes and I knew he wished that he had sired him, not me. I hated my cousin with the wholehearted animosity that always accompanies jealousy, particularly in a child's mind. He was a year younger than me, robust and proud, and never slow to take advantage of my father's fondness for him. When no one was looking, he would push me hard so that I would topple over to the ground and scream in frustrated rage. One of my maids would hasten to put me back on my feet but my day would have been ruined anyway. If I tried to get my own back on him by telling tales, my father would frown, his brow thunderous, and motion for me to be quiet. And Vigraha would look hurt and injured but throw me a threatening look from under his lashes. This was the way it always was.

3

By the time I was ten, I knew what I had suspected all along—that my father hated me and was ashamed to acknowledge me as his daughter. A ruler of his stature should have had a strong, healthy son to his name, after all, not a weakling girl who was lame. I also knew that there was some sort of tension between my parents, a simmering hostility. At first, I thought I was the sole cause but I soon came to realize that it was more complex than that. My mother was from the powerful Shahi family of Gandhara and had married into Lohara, as was the tacit tradition between the two royal houses.

It was doomed to failure, though—this mismatched union between my forceful, ambitious mother and my short-tempered, indolent father. The more my father frittered away his time and money on drunken pursuits and sycophants, the more frustrated my mother grew. I had often heard her berate him for behaving in a manner unbecoming of a ruler of Lohara, but only heard his jeers in response. The taunts must have worsened after my birth, I suppose. The more brusque and dismissive my father was of me, the more tender and loving were my mother's attentions. Yet, was I a failure, even though my mother tried hard to conceal it? Had she, perhaps, bribed the astrologer to make his prediction about me?

My mother's father, the Shahi ruler of Gandhara, was a formidable figure. But his harsh expression would instantly soften when he set eyes on me. I always looked forward to his visits to Lohara, which were, fortunately, frequent. Whenever he clattered into the palace courtyard with his entourage, I would run from my chamber to greet him and promptly get swung in the air in dizzying circles while he exclaimed over me. When I was with him, no one and nothing could touch me or mar my happiness, not even my father's sulky expression and ill-concealed annoyance.

That I was dear to my grandfather was known all over the court. It was something that even Vigraha was forced to acknowledge. He usually skulked in the corner, unseen, during these visits.

On one of these visits, when I was about ten and beginning to learn some things about myself—my quick temper, my curiosity about the world of men, my intelligence and beauty that people were starting to notice—as I ran past him, full of excitement, Vigraha hissed at me, 'Your grandfather's so old, he will drop dead very soon.'

'Come and say it to his face,' I challenged him, laughing at the fear in his eyes that had sprung up, unbidden.

Later, I curled up on my grandfather's lap in my mother's private chamber, snug in the circle of his huge, hairy arms. He asked me to recite any verses that I had recently learnt and when I did, he praised my progress lavishly, my mother's face mirroring his pride.

'Learning is wasted on a girl,' my father snarled, 'particularly one who will never even use her skills to attract a good match.'

My grandfather frowned. 'Learning is never wasted on an astute mind such as Didda's,' he retorted. 'And anyone would be fortunate to marry the daughter of Simharaja of Lohara and the granddaughter of Bhima Shahi.'

'The *lame* daughter of Simharaja of Lohara,' my father pointed out, causing sudden tears to spring in my eyes and my grandfather's face to darken in rage. From the way my mother was twisting her hands in her lap, I knew she was outraged as well but probably thought it wise to contain her anger.

My grandfather thrust me gently from his lap and motioned me towards the door. 'I will see you in a while,' he said softly. 'Go to your chamber now.'

As I limped out of the room, I heard him say, 'Your daughter, who happens to be lame, is destined for greatness. Or don't you trust the words of your own astrologer?'

I didn't hear my father's reply but I knew from experience that it would be sullen and spiteful, full of venom towards my mother or me. He didn't believe his astrologer any more than I did, after all.

As always, my grandfather's visit ended all too soon, just at the point when I had begun to greet each new day with the anticipation of his delightful presence. This time, though, he had saved me a surprise for last, a gift, as it were.

On the morning of his departure, he led me by the hand to the stables. I wrinkled my nose at the smell of dung and horse sweat emanating from there and tugged at his sleeve. 'Why are we going here? You know I am scared of horses.'

He guffawed. 'You shouldn't be, my little Didda.'

'But they're so big and they snort so loudly and I'm afraid they'll kick me,' I wailed, trying to wrest my hand from his grip.

'Wait till you see what I have for you,' he promised and my curiosity got the better of me, so I trotted along beside him, unresisting.

We had barely taken a few more steps when a burly man emerged from the stable door, leading a tall, thin boy, who looked about my age, by the hand just as my grandfather led me. Both of them bowed reverentially to us.

'Is he ready? Have you told him?' asked my grandfather.

'Yes, sire. He is ready.'

'Didda, this is my master-of-horse, Varuna,' explained my grandfather, 'and this is his son, Naravahana. He is to stay back here at the palace and help with the horses. And maybe he can teach you to ride one. Wouldn't you like that?'

I stiffened. 'I told you I don't like horses,' I muttered, so that only my grandfather would hear.

Naravahana stepped forward, his face mobile with enthusiasm. 'Princess, it would be an honour to help you,' he said. 'Horses are gentle, loyal animals, you will see.'

I stared at him, taking in his light brown eyes, thick hair and pleasing smile, and all at once, before I quite knew it, I found myself smiling back and nodding.

My grandfather laughed and clapped my shoulder. 'No tears when I leave now, I suppose? I told you that you'd like my surprise!'

We stood side by side, Naravahana and I, while my grandfather and his entourage wheeled down the palace drive and out of the massive gates. I glanced at Naravahana and found him looking a trifle woebegone.

'Will you miss your father?' I demanded, with more curiosity than tact.

He nodded his head, his face miserable. Was he actually going to *cry*?

'Well, he'll be back soon,' I said briskly, trying to forestall his tears. 'Meanwhile, we have lots to do. I can show you around the entire palace—and it's huge!—and then we can explore the forest and the lake and play games. Oh and then you can show me how to ride a horse and ...' With this, my voice faltered but I had managed to distract him successfully for he chuckled. His laugh was infectious and I found myself giggling helplessly. He followed suit and then we had to hold our aching sides, gasping for breath as we grinned at each other.

'You really don't want to ride, do you, princess?'

I shook my head and giggled. Thus did Naravahana and I become friends.

VALGA

I hated Lohara on sight—its palace, its people, its trees, its food, virtually everything about it. And yet, I knew this was because I pined for my home in the tiny village near Udabhanda, the capital city of Gandhara—the place where I was born and took my first steps and said my first words.

I had begged and pleaded with my parents to be allowed to stay, till my throat grew hoarse, but no one listened, no one at all. My mother tried to be stoic but the tears coursed down her cheeks in an unending cascade when she thought I wasn't looking. She kept her face turned away towards the cooking pot but I was not fooled. I cuddled my sisters and my new baby brother and thought my heart would surely break into several shards if I left them and went away.

'Let me stay and I'll do all the cooking and cleaning and every single chore in the house,' I coaxed my mother. 'I can do it, you know I can—you've always said I'm so strong.' When my mother didn't reply, I burst out, 'Why are you sending me away? Do you hate me?'

At that, my mother heaved a sob and buried me in her embrace. I breathed in her familiar smell of cinnamon and wood-smoke and found myself heaving with sobs as well. I knew there was nothing she could do; that she was as helpless in the matter as I. There were just too many mouths to feed—that was the stark fact—and so, I had to be sent away to make it easier on those who remained.

It wasn't any surprise that my father had picked on me thus. I knew he had no affection for me, his eldest daughter. His eyes sparkled with derision and anger whenever they rested on me. Perhaps part of the reason was that my heavy features bore no semblance of beauty and he knew I would never make a good match. I am short and stout, my broad face unremarkable, my black hair hanging limply down my back. I do not have anything of my mother's delicate beauty or my father's chiselled features. The only remarkable thing about me is that I am very strong. I can chop wood with the heavy axe effortlessly, and fetch and carry for hours on end without tiring.

And now, this was the justification for sending me away. I was to make myself useful in my aunt's quarters in the palace complex of Lohara where she was a seamstress. She needed someone to help cook and clean as she was getting on in years, and that was to be my job. In return, I would have a roof over my head and food to eat—a very generous offer, in her view. Yet I knew my aunt's nature and had always detested her. Her temper tantrums, usually directed at my helpless mother on her occasional visits to our dilapidated home, would leave me shaking with rage and pent-up resentment. Yet there was nothing I could do for my father always sided with his sister and, in any case, I was afraid of unlocking his violent streak. Now I was to be at her mercy and the thought filled me with anxiety.

The day slated for my departure came all too soon, and caught me unprepared and miserable. I was to accompany a soldier, a friend of my father, who was in King Bhima Shahi's army, and who had agreed to escort me to Lohara in exchange for a few coins. The king made frequent visits to his daughter in Lohara and so, there was nothing unusual about this journey except that there was a girl in the midst of his entourage whose throat was choked with rage and tears, and whose heart was full of hatred— hatred towards a world that decreed that a daughter must obey her father in all things even if he banished her from the only home and family she knew.

I had made my farewells the night before. Many tears had been shed and many vows to meet anon had been exchanged but I knew the truth: that I would never see my family again and would have to live the rest of my life wondering if my mother was well and if my sister would grow strong like me and if my baby brother would ever know that he had an older sister called Valga.

I didn't see my father until it was time to leave and then he suddenly turned up to pull me roughly down the track leading to the main street where his friend awaited us. A minute later and I had a temporary guardian who hoisted my small bundle on to his shoulder and pointed in the direction of the big town of Udabhanda where the palace was. This was where the troop would leave from.

I looked at my father, my mind seething with emotions. 'Look after my mother,' I began, trying to keep my voice from trembling, 'and—'

'Don't tell me what to do, girl,' he snarled. 'You behave well in your aunt's house or I'll know.'

I whipped my face away and began to walk towards the town, following in the soldiers's footsteps. So much for a father's love! In that moment, I wished he would drop down and die but I wasn't to know then that this would soon come to pass. Some weeks later, I got to know that he had been killed in a drunken brawl on the outskirts of our village. I did not know what became of my mother and my family. I wondered if I would ever see them again.

I'm standing now on the banks of a stream whose water is so clear, so luminous, that I can see every detail of my face reflected in it just as if I were holding up a mirror to my face. There are trees around me whose branches droop down to the water and brush back and forth in the slight wind that sometimes sends a small shower of drops onto me. Lohara probably looks her best in the summer, I think, and this place is the best of all. It is my retreat from the world when my aunt has been particularly vicious to me—and that is nearly every day, these days.

It has been a month since I was foisted into her care and she has never let me forget it. She works me to the bone, hardly caring whether I am sick or weary, and feeds me just enough to keep me going. I am made to clean every corner of the house, sometimes several times a day—and then to cook all manner of dishes that I barely get to savour since they instantly disappear down her greedy throat. She has even forced me into doing a large part of her sewing and stitching—work that I loathe—and the skin of my fingers is now hard and bruised where she has driven the needle into it when I have been clumsy or slow to comprehend the task at hand. I hate her with a slow, burning hatred that is beginning to consume my mind. I think she knows it, too, and that is why she constantly punishes me with her acerbic tongue and impossible tasks.

I am drawn from my reverie by a shout from the farther side of the stream that is obscured from me by a curve in its bed. It is the side nearer the palace, the side

13

that I avoid, but I can't contain my curiosity as the sounds grow more strident and urgent. Those are clearly shouts of help—and is that ... mocking laughter?

I step around the bend in the bank and come upon a strange sight. Princess Didda—for I know it is her, having observed her from afar on several occasions—is sprawled in an ungainly manner on the ground and struggling to get to her feet, crying in rage. Yet her short, portly cousin, the one they call Prince Vigraharaja, knocks her down whenever she manages to raise herself. The ground is wet and sticky with mud, and her clothes are soiled with it.

I look around for help but there is no one in sight; we are completely alone. Anger flares in my mind and, before I quite know what I'm doing, I rush across and knock the boy off his feet. He falls to the ground with an outraged shout but springs up at once and races at me. He is surprisingly swift despite his bulk.

I try to run but he grabs my cloak and whips me around to face him so sharply that my neck throbs with pain. Then he slaps me across my cheek and punches me in the chest.

'How dare you!' he screams, his fists clenched, his thick eyebrows meeting above his eyes in one straight line. 'How dare you touch me, you ugly, low-caste, filthy servant, you—'

He doesn't complete the sentence because I have punched him back in the chest and he must be completely winded because he collapses with a groan and falls silent. Trying to ignore the pain in my neck and chest and cheek, I hold out a hand to the princess and more or less haul her to her feet. She stands, leaning heavily on me, and panting as if she has run for miles.

Then she says, 'I thank you, whoever you are. In a minute he would have thrown me into the water and then I wouldn't have known what to do.'

'Can't you swim, Princess Didda?' I ask without thinking and then wish I could bite out my tongue for I have suddenly remembered she is lame. My face grows red and I stammer, 'I ... I'm sorry. That was stupid of me.'

She does not ask me how I know her name or her disability. I suppose she takes it for granted that both are common knowledge. I find myself wondering what it would be like to be so famous, so well-known, the princess of an entire kingdom of people.

All of a sudden, I find her steering me towards the stream, still leaning on me for support. We gaze down into the water, the unruffled surface reflecting our solemn faces faithfully, her big, black eyes staring at mine, her long black hair swinging like a rope. We stand there for a while, trying to get back our breath, but we have grown careless, for I hear a twig snap behind us.

When I whirl around, Prince Vigraharaja is right behind and advancing menacingly, with the clear intention of pushing us into the stream.

Panic seizes me—the princess can't swim and I would be weighed down in the water if she sank and dragged me with her. Unless . . .

In a swift, fluid movement, I grasp the princess around her waist, hoist her onto my shoulders and enter the stream just out of reach of the prince's long fingers. The water is cold despite it being summer and the shock makes me gasp but then I steady myself and begin to strike out for the other side, the princess clinging on to my head for dear life. Within a couple of minutes, we are safe on the other bank with the prince dancing in frustration on the opposite side. Even before I lay her gently on the ground, Princess Didda is laughing as if she will never stop—great, deep chuckles that shake her body and bring tears to her eyes.

'How did you do that, my dear friend?' she asks, once her laughter has worked its way out of her.

I am torn between pride and fear. I have managed to rescue a princess but the look on her cousin's face tells me he will not forgive—or forget. I ignore my worries and smile at her. 'I am strong,' I say simply, 'and I didn't know how else to stop him.'

'Your name?' she asks, suddenly thoughtful.

'Valga.'

'You live here, Valga?'

'My aunt is your seamstress. I live with her.'

'Tell your aunt that you have a new job from today. Will you do that?' she orders.

My breath quickens. New job? What does the princess mean?

'You will carry me around, Valga,' she says confidently, as if she knows I won't argue with her. 'You will be with me at all times to make sure that my limp doesn't hinder me. Will you do that for me, Valga?'

Once again, I find myself stammering but it is a rush of happiness that is stemming my words. 'Princess ... Princess ... I would be honoured. I ...'

She turns away from me abruptly and shouts across to her cousin. 'Don't you dare hurt Valga again! She's a friend—and she serves me now.'

He shakes his fist at us and storms off to the palace. I am feeling slightly dizzy. Too much has happened too fast. Am I now a friend of a *princess*?

I breathe in deeply and find Princess Didda regarding me with an amused air. 'Come, let's go in,' she says. 'I will introduce you to my mother and then you will have to shift into my chambers at once. Your aunt will *have* to agree, of course.'

I trail along in the wake of my new, royal friend, hardly able to believe that my fortunes have changed so suddenly and so dramatically. Will I be accepted by the queen, by the royal family, as an appropriate companion to the princess? Will I be able to fulfil the duties required of me? Is this why destiny has made me so strong—so that I can be the carrier-girl of a princess?

My mind is swimming with questions and thoughts and so, I pay no attention to the most important fact of all in what has transpired, one that is to haunt me several years later: that what Princess Didda wants, she gets—and nothing and no one can stand in her way.

OF SONS AND DAUGHTERS

DIDDA

I look in the mirror and view my image with critical eyes. A tall girl—almost a woman—with big, dark eyes looks back at me. She has long, curly hair that falls down to her waist and a wide brow with prominent cheekbones and thick, arched eyebrows. Her nose is neither long nor short but is perfectly shaped with delicately-flared nostrils. Her mouth is pretty, too, although her front teeth are slightly prominent. In this, I have taken after my father—the only aspect that openly links me to him. In everything else, I am the image of my mother. I think I am beautiful and, indeed, my maids tell me so openly.

Yet when I take a step or two forward and my lame foot drags behind the other, I know I look ungainly and distinctly ugly—and there is nothing I can do to change it. A succession of physicians has examined me, seeking to find a cure to my disability, but all to no avail. My lameness is an intrinsic part of me, an extension of my identity. It will never go away.

Is this why no one wants to marry me? I am sixteen and proposals have been sent far and wide for my hand but they are all turned down. I know the reason why—I am not stupid. Who would want to marry a lame woman, however beautiful she may be, and ruin their lives with a crippled partner? If I were a man, I, too, might not have wanted to marry a woman such as I. So there is no one to blame but my fate, my harsh destiny, which brands me as unsuitable in a world that has fixed ideals of beauty and desirability. I should reconcile myself to the fact that I will never marry, never bear children, never have a family of my own. Perhaps my future greatness will derive from this depressing fact.

'Don't you want to get married someday?' I ask Naravahana and his fair skin is immediately suffused with colour. He turns his eyes on me and looks at me for a while, wordlessly. It has been some years since we met at the palace stables and we spend most of our time together now, talking, strolling, playing and keeping each other company. We are so comfortable with each other that I can invariably read his thoughts and so, I know what is in his mind, at this point. 'Oh, yes, I know,' I laugh. 'You want to marry me someday, don't you?'

'I … I wouldn't dare to … it would be an honour beyond …' He is so awkward and embarrassed that I should stop right now but some perverse instinct makes me want to taunt him further. The intervening years have changed me but he still looks like an overgrown boy with long limbs and a shambling gait that often seems to be accentuated by shyness. Yet he has also shown surprising courage and confidence, particularly when Vigraharaja harasses me. He has sometimes been beaten black-and-blue by my cousin but he obstinately defends me and stands up for me.

'Some day I will marry a king and go off to a faraway land,' I remark cruelly. 'What will you do then?'

'I will follow you,' he says simply. 'I will go wherever you go.'

I click my tongue in impatience and pretend not to care but I am touched by his assertion. He hasn't yet taught me to ride—and probably never will!—but there is something in his personality that draws me to him, perhaps his stillness or his patience. I am mercurial, short-tempered and sometimes arrogant—I know this of myself. He is the exact opposite of what I am and this is true of Valga, too. She is stoic, quiet and ever obliging, strong in mind and body. Although I never tell them so, I am glad of their company, these two friends of mine. I laugh with them but also at them—yet they never take offence but continue to serve me and for this, I am truly grateful. I wish, sometimes, that I could be like them but I am destined for greatness and so, I *have* to be different.

My days pass in an unvarying routine of studies and chores. I delight in my learning and devour the texts that my teacher hands me. He says I have a very quick brain and am able to grasp difficult concepts effortlessly. I glow in his praise and my mother compliments me, too, but my father remains as distant as ever. He is gentler with my mother nowadays, though, for she is expecting another child. She has miscarried several times in the past few years but this time around, the physician is hopeful.

'She had better bear a full-term son,' my father tells him in his usual surly tone. We are at the door of my mother's chambers, and the physician has just stepped outside after conversing with her and the midwife. He bows low and nods, while my stomach contracts with anger.

How dare my father speak of my poor mother thus! It is not her fault that she has miscarried before. Before I can stop myself, I step forward. 'My mother cannot help it if she loses her babies,' I say hotly.

My father looks at me, not bothering to conceal the disgust on his face. 'Shut your mouth,' he retorts, almost as if he is spitting out the words. 'I'll not have you interfering in matters that don't concern you, you hear me?'

I am shamed and made to feel stupid before the physician and some courtiers who are passing by and who have clearly overheard this tirade. My face burns with anger and fury makes me reckless. 'I am your daughter, not some worthless servant,' I exclaim. 'Why do you talk to me like this?'

A sneer spreads across my father's features. 'But that's *exactly* what you are to me—worthless.'

I am trembling so much in rage that I feel as if I will collapse onto the floor but Valga tugs at my hand and gently pulls me along to my chamber. Naravahana, released momentarily from the stables, runs alongside.

'He hates me,' I cry, choking on the tears that are flowing down my cheeks. 'Isn't a father supposed to love his daughter? Why does he behave like this?'

Valga soothes me, looking extremely stricken as if she is struggling with a sorrow of her own. I briefly wonder what it is but then submit myself to her ministrations. She holds me in her strong arms and rocks me till my tears cease and I feel better. Worn out, I fall asleep only to wake later and find her sitting by my side, looking at me anxiously. I think she has been crying as well for her cheeks are stained with tears but I am too full of my own grievances to question her. She rises wordlessly when I get to my feet and follows me out of the palace.

We go for a long walk along the stream, my cheeks cooling rapidly in the crisp autumn breeze. My stomach feels hollow and I realise I haven't eaten anything since my morning meal. I continue walking, though—I don't want to face anyone else from the palace just yet.

Naravahana joins us after a while. As always, Valga falls behind a little and he begins to match my slow steps to his, talking about the latest horse to join our stables and the long ride that he went on the other day along the banks of the lake. His chatter is soporific; listening to it, I am soothed. Valga reaches out a hand to steady me every now and then when sharp obstacles crop up in my path, keeping me from stumbling. I relax completely in the company of my friends. It has always been so. Whenever I am agitated or upset, my worries drift away when I am with them.

Later, I look in on my mother. The curtains in her room are drawn against the sunlight. A fire roars in a corner and the air is stifling. Within minutes, I am bathed in sweat and I wonder how she can bear the heat.

'Are you cold?' I ask, tucking the covers around her swollen body.

She smiles and draws me to her. 'Don't argue with your father, Didda. It will only make you miserable and him, angry.'

She must have overheard us earlier. I stiffen, anger flooding my mind all over again. 'He doesn't care about you,' I complain. 'He only wants a child, a full-term one, even if you die in the process!'

'Hush! I am not going to die, my dearest. And, after all, he does want a son, an heir, to rule after him.'

'Why can't I be his heir?' I ask mutinously.

'A woman doesn't rule, Didda. Only a man can occupy a throne. You know that.'

I am struck anew by the unfairness of the world that relegates women to an inferior place and, at the same time, treats men like gods. Why should it be this way? If I don't get a brother, then Vigraha will rule Lohara after my father—and what kind of a ruler would he be with his perversity and malice and cruelty? He is a very poor scholar as well—I have overheard the teacher telling my father so several times. In that case, wouldn't I make a better ruler with my brains and my abilities? Wasn't this clear to everyone? Then why were they turning a blind eye to it? I feel terribly frustrated but a part of me knows that there is precious little I can do about it.

In the months that follow, I am wracked by anxiety about my mother, for whom it is a difficult pregnancy. She remains confined to her bed, struggling to pass the days till her confinement. Worry assails me every single day

25

and there are times when I feel I can't breathe from the sheer oppressive weight of it. My nights are filled with dreams of her death and I wake, trembling, grasping at reality with both hands.

It is at times like these that I am truly grateful, all over again, for my two friends who seem to sense my moods as soon as they near me and devise all manner of distractions to make me get through them all. With Naravahana, it is his gentle chatter about his beloved horses; with Valga, it is her silent sympathy that almost has a physical presence.

My father, meanwhile, is often away from Lohara and it is his ministers who rule in his stead these days. I don't know what his business is outside his realm but I do know that an absentee ruler speedily translates into trouble for his kingdom. They say that he is meeting other rulers, transacting treaties with them and fighting hard to maintain the prevailing power equations. Yet in his absence, most of his ministers are pitted against each other, vying for greater wealth and favours, and my mother often has to resolve their arguments that prove intractable.

She invariably sends me away if I am with her at the time, but my ears are sharp and there is no one to see me standing just by the door to her room, half-concealed by the thick, embroidered curtains that more or less obscure it. I have learned a lot just by listening and observing, and the knowledge I have gained thereby of statecraft and political ploys fills me with excitement and makes me long to plunge into these discussions and voice my opinion.

Vigraha catches me once while I am lurking by her door and seizes my arm, his eyes gleaming.

'I'll tell your father what you do,' he smirks, pulling me away roughly. 'Don't think I haven't been watching you all this while!'

My lame foot hurts where he's dragged it over the stone floor and his fingers dig painfully into my arm. I try to wrest it from his grip but he is stronger than me and I find I can't do so. And then, I am flooded with violent rage, as I frequently am, and kick out blindly with my other leg, so that he jerks back with a cry of pain, releasing my bruised arm. The marks of his fingers are red against my skin and I hate him so much at this moment, that I feel I will burst with it.

'I'll tell my father what you did with his horse,' I vow, incensed.

His eyes momentarily fill with fear and I know my words have struck home. I am probably the only one who knows what he did because it involved Naravahana and there is little that the latter conceals from me. I have been wondering what to do with this knowledge for over a fortnight but now I know exactly how to use it.

'You and your love-struck dog!' he mutters with venom and then he pushes past me and is gone. I take a deep breath and nurse my arm as I recall Naravahana's fury as he had narrated the incident to me.

Vigraha had stalked into the stables one day and demanded that one of my father's favourite horses, a black charger, be saddled for him. Naravahana, who was helping to groom the horses—his daily chore—had promptly refused, knowing that Vigraha was taking undue advantage of his uncle's absence. Vigraha, furious, swore at Naravahana and tried to hit him. Naravahana parried the stroke but was unable to prevent Vigraha from jumping on to the charger and riding him out of the stables in a mad gallop.

They had been away for hours and Naravahana had fretted over the horse's disappearance for he loved the beast just as he did all the other stable animals. His fears were fully realised when the charger was returned exhausted, covered with foamy sweat and bleeding from gashes inflicted by Vigraha's whip. The hapless beast, trembling and worn, was tended to by a weeping Naravahana who came to me with the sorry tale just as soon as the horse had fallen asleep.

'You must tell your father,' he had begged me. 'I would, but he might not believe my word against that of your cousin.'

'And he'll believe mine?' I mocked. 'Are you blind, my friend?'

'You should try, princess,' he said earnestly. 'What if he does this again when your father isn't there?'

'All right, I will,' I promised. 'Just as soon as he returns.'

And yet, when my father does return, I am unable to tell him what has transpired in his absence, I am unable to say anything at all, for he silences me with a statement. He summons my mother and me to him, and then tells me curtly, 'You are to be married to the king of Kashmira. Make your preparations.'

My mother raises her head sharply. 'To Kshemagupta of Kashmira? When did you ...'

'It is a trade-off.' My father's words cut through hers. 'He gets Didda, I get a little land. It isn't much—but, after all, a cripple has no value.'

A cold fear settles around my heart and I stare at my father, dumbfounded. I can hear my mother's voice raised in anger, in indignation. I can hear my father shouting in reply. I can't make out the words, though, because a different set is echoing round and round my brain. It says: 'You are being sold, Didda. Your father has sold you for a paltry bit of land.'

VALGA

She is to be married and this is the wrong choice for her; I know it is. I have been listening to the servants and courtiers of the palace and there has been enough said about the king of Kashmira for me to fear for Didda and her future. I have discussed this with Naravahana, too, and he is pale with anxiety for her.

It seems Kshemagupta is a pleasure-loving fool with an army of flatterers who ensure that he spends all the money in the treasury. His father, Parvagupta, was a ruthless man who pretended to support the previous king but upstaged him after lulling him into complacency. Parvagupta committed countless murders to get at the throne before finally dying a violent death. They say his prime minister, Phalguna, has now taken over his mantle. He keeps watch over Kshemagupta and encourages his dissolute ways because the real power often emanates from him, rather than the king. And here is the worst blow of all to Didda: Phalguna has married his daughter, Chandralekha, to Kshemagupta and so, she will only have the status of a second wife.

I mull over these facts and then wonder if Didda knows about them. Should I forewarn her, let her prepare herself for a life of inevitable subordination and frustration? Or should I maintain my silence and let her enjoy some days of mental peace before she steps into her new life? I have this fierce desire to protect her from her problems—and I have realised that Naravahana and I are at one on this. For Didda inspires loyalty and warmth, and, I, for one, have fallen under her spell—the charm of her laughter, the warmth of her friendship, the fire of her generosity. She is good to me, treats me well, showers me with gifts—all this in return for carrying her around at games, supporting her when she walks, being by her side to lend an arm if she is tired. I am happier than I have ever been before. And yet, I am not insensible to her faults. I know that her temper is ugly, that she can often be selfish and self-absorbed, that she is stubborn to the point of exasperation.

I am brooding, seeking a way out of my dilemma, when I hear a commotion near the queen's chambers and I know, without being expressly told, that her child is on its way. I can hear her maids screaming for the midwife, an elderly, stooped woman with surprisingly large hands whom I have seen in the palace many a time. I rise to my feet reluctantly and make my way to the queen's side to see whether I am needed. As it happens, there are too many grim-faced minions attending on her and so, I decide to go where I am needed most—to Didda's side.

She is in her chamber, idly tracing her quill over a page and I hesitate at the doorway, uncertain whether she desires my company right now.

'Come in, Valga,' she says without turning her head. Over the years, she has come to sense my presence without my making a single sound to alert her.

'It is your mother's time,' I say gently and she nods. Then she looks at me, her big eyes so full of apprehension that I long to reassure her. But I remain my usual silent self.

'If I have a sister, my father will ...' Her voice trails off but we both know what she wants to say. If the queen has another girl, King Simharaja might dissolve his marriage with her or worse. He might even kill the infant—and how is it her fault, I wonder with a lump in my throat. Unbidden, images of my father fill my mind but I try to push them away to a corner.

'You should pray then, princess,' I say firmly. 'Ask Goddess Sharada for what you seek.'

Her laugh is bitter. 'If the goddess truly listened to me, would I be a cripple?'

The entire night passes and we maintain a sort of weary vigil, hoping for news. The sun is well into the sky the following day before we are told that the child has been born and it does not require a feat of intelligence to discern its sex from the beaming face of the queen's servant. I am walking with Didda and Naravahana on the shores of the lake but we turn as one and head for the palace. I take Didda's weight on my strong shoulders and walk as fast as I can but she urges me to go even faster. Naravahana looks excited and I am sure I resemble him in this. The princess is expressionless, her face blank, but her voice rings with relief and happiness.

The queen is lying on her bed, looking wan and exhausted. The heat in her room is suffocating; the great fire has been banked up with so much wood that it bellows like an animal in the corner. I wipe the beads of sweat off my face and watch from a respectful distance as Didda throws herself on her mother and embraces her. The baby is in the old midwife's arms. Its face is obscured by heavy folds of cloth and all I can glimpse from where I stand is a fair cheek.

'Can I hold him?' Didda asks and the baby is lowered carefully into her waiting arms. She laughs and croons to the child, rocking him slightly. The queen laughs as she watches her two children with pride.

All at once, there is an angry shout from the doorway. I smell the king before I see him—a reek of horses and sweat—and sink to my knees as does everyone else. He marches up to Didda and seizes the child from her. 'You fool!' he rages at the midwife. 'Giving my precious son to a cripple to hold? If she had dropped him, I would have had your head. Do you understand that?'

'Why are you making a fuss?' The queen's voice is weak, yet the sharp tone in it doesn't escape the king. 'Didda—'

'I don't want to hear about Didda,' he snaps. 'All I am interested in is my son. My own son and heir at last!'

I steal a glance at Didda. Her face is wooden but her clenched fists announce her fury. She draws herself up to her full height and walks regally out of the room, and I follow in her wake. Naravahana is hovering by the door and looks stricken; clearly, he has overheard the king. He follows us as usual.

Didda doesn't stop until she reaches the stream and it is there that she allows the mask to slip. Grief and resentment are writ large on her face.

'I love him,' she says abruptly. 'My little brother.'

We nod and my heart aches with sympathy. 'My father wanted a son, too,' I venture. 'And he was all that my father cared about.'

Naravahana clears his throat. 'My father doesn't want me either,' he says stiffly, as if the words have touched the air for the first time. 'He married after my mother died and had a son with his new wife. So that's why he left me in Lohara.'

So each of us has a similar tale of sorrow behind our smiles! And we are bound by this in some strange way. Naravahana and I have never really spoken much to each other over the years of our acquaintance because Didda is always there with us and commands our attention. Nevertheless, I feel closer to him now than ever. Perhaps he senses it, too, for he smiles ruefully at me and nods slightly.

And then we turn to Didda. She is in some sort of reverie; I don't think she has heard either of us. For a while longer, she is silent and then she motions the two of us to walk with her up the lake path towards the hill that overlooks it. The crest of the hill is often used as a vantage point by the palace guards because it provides a clear view of the surrounding areas—even all the way north to Kashmira. There is a straight track that bisects the hill and leads to the crest, and this is the one that we follow. We have climbed the hill several times before but now there is a new urgency to Didda's steps.

I hold on to her firmly, carrying her when the terrain turns rough and supporting her over the grassier parts. It takes a while but we struggle and pant and sweat all the way to the top. The land flattens out here like the lid of a plateau and Naravahana flops on to the grass. Didda, on the other hand, shrugs off my restraining arm and limps over to the very edge. I beckon to Naravahana and we stand on either side of her, following her gaze.

Torn white clouds float lazily over our heads and there in the distance towards the north, half-shrouded in mist, lies the immense valley of Kashmira. It is too distant to see clearly but we shade our eyes and look on silently. It appears small and compact from here but I know that what we see is only a fraction of its real size, and it is, in fact, several times the size of Lohara. It is, indeed, larger and more powerful than each of the kingdoms that surround it and it dominates them all. Lohara, Rajapuri, Parnotsa and all the others are like mere ants before the majestic lion of Kashmira.

'My destiny awaits me there.' Didda breaks the silence. 'And I will seize it with both hands.' She pauses and then her voice grows louder. 'I'll show him,' she says. 'I will fulfil my destiny. Greatness awaits me.' She repeats this over and over, each time more shrilly, until what issues from her lips is a scream.

Naravahana and I fall back slightly, awed by the power and conviction in her tone. A flock of birds, startled by the sounds, streams from the branches of a nearby tree and wheels sharply into the air. The sky fills with the fluttering of wings—and then there is silence.

And into the silence, she screams.

ENDINGS AND BEGINNINGS

DIDDA

Vigraha is even more insufferable than usual. He is jealous of my baby brother, Udayaraja, who will now inherit the throne of Lohara after my father. Yet he also takes equal delight in the fact that I have been shown my 'proper place'. He stops me one day when I am on my way to my daily lesson by lunging forward and twisting my arm. I struggle furiously and he is forced to relax his grip and let go but he backs me into a corner all the same and pens me in.

I look around for help and curse the fact that Valga isn't with me today. Her aunt had summoned her for some urgent chore and I had allowed her to go. I kick out with my good foot but Vigraha sidesteps it neatly and laughs. His thick eyebrows twist in a mocking dance on his brow.

'You might as well have not been born, *Princess* Didda,' he jeers. 'As far as your parents are concerned, they have only one child—and he is a boy.'

'My mother loves me,' I cry before I can stop myself and then wish I could lure the words back into my mouth.

A smug smile spreads across his face at my discomfiture. 'But your father doesn't, does he?' he asks softly. 'And he is the king. And your mother is sworn to obey him. And she has given him a son. So she has made up for her mistake in having you.'

I hear the welcome sound of footsteps and then Naravahana runs up to us. He has recently been given some additional duties at court and so, he is more often in the palace these days than in the stables.

His light eyes are now glazed with anger and he plucks at Vigraha's back. 'Let the princess go.'

'I am talking to my cousin about family matters,' snaps Vigraha, 'so don't you dare interrupt.'

Naravahana bristles but he wisely holds his silence. He is prudent but I am not. 'Let's talk about *you*, Vigraha' I retort. 'You'll never become king now, will you? You will have to spend your life serving my brother just as you serve my father now.'

I see his eyes flash with anger. He raises a hand as if to strike me but I do not flinch. Naravahana makes a sound of protest. Vigraha steps aside and pulls me roughly into the corridor.

'So speaks someone whose only value is to be sold for land,' he snarls. 'Your father has made a good bargain. He has given away something of no worth to get something infinitely more valuable. He is a wise king indeed.'

I limp away as fast as I can from him, away from his hateful slurs. Naravahana follows me, anxious to heal my wound with his words—as is the way between friends—but there is nothing he can do or say to placate me.

We go down to the stream and I pace its bank till my anger has abated slightly. Then I turn to him and say, 'Find out as much as you can. What is my marriage bargain all about? What exactly has my father gained in exchange for me?'

He nods and bows, and then leaves my presence in his usual unobtrusive way. I return to my chamber and wait for him but the minutes turn into hours and he does not appear. While I wait, I lift the hem of my long silk skirt and examine my foot—its crooked shape, its odd angle. And then I examine the other—its perfect shape and symmetry. How can it be that they belong to the same body? How can something so flawless exist alongside something so malformed? And yet, even as I think this, I know that it is the same with my mind. One part is normal, even good—it craves love and support and encouragement, it shuns evil and looks towards truth and virtue, it wants happiness for others and for myself.

But the other part? I think I have known all along that I am prey to frightening emotions and impulses; that my outward beauty cloaks something very dangerous within. It is this that makes me want to harm my father for harming me with his actions, to wound Vigraha for wounding me with his words, to maul the world for mauling me with its indifference because I am not a man. It is power that I want—the power to be acknowledged and respected for who I am, the power to crush those who taunt and humiliate me, the power to command those who dismiss me as a cripple and sell me to the highest bidder for land. I see this now with complete clarity.

Naravahana comes before me and fractures my thoughts. Dusk has fallen and as the lamps have not yet been lit in my chamber, his face—and mine—are in shadow. I am suddenly grateful for this simple fact. Perhaps I do not want this dear friend of mine to read the naked emotions on my face.

'Thirty-six villages,' he says without preamble.

'From where? Whose were they?'

'They belonged to the Jayendravihara—it's a famous monastery of the Buddhists in Kashmira.' He pauses and then resumes his tale carefully. 'King Kshemagupta burnt it down when the Buddhists in the vihara gave refuge to a landlord, Sangrama, who had refused to pay his taxes. The king melted down the Buddha image that was enshrined within and then used the brass in a temple of his own, the Kshemagaurishvara.' He pauses again and looks me in the eye. 'He gave the villages to your father in return for all his help. And in return for you.'

So my future husband is a violent, religious bigot who is clearly devoid of all mercy. What has my father been helping him with? How has it led to this bargain? And did Kshemagupta ask for me on his own? Or did my father offer me as a sacrifice to keep him happy and ensure his continued generosity?

Naravahana clears his throat. 'There is more, princess,' he says, his face carefully emptied of all emotion. 'They say King Kshemagupta drinks and his degenerate friends lead him astray. All the power is in the prime minister, Phalguna's hands, who is secure in the fact that the king has married his daughter.' My heart lurches. I force myself to continue listening but it seems that Naravahana has nothing more to say.

In a few simple words, though, he has wrecked my vision of the future and any dreams I might have nurtured. Is this to be the basis of my greatness? Will my fame spread on account of being the most unfortunate girl in Lohara?

I feel tears coming but I force them away. They are a sign of weakness and I will be strong, I *will*. I will take this poor destiny in my hands and turn it around. And I will not let anyone or anything stand in the way.

All of Lohara is humming with activity. The preparations for my marriage are under way and the days that remain for me in my childhood home are fast trickling away. Every available and able body has been pressed into service for decorating the palace, acquiring the requisite provisions, and making and overseeing the arrangements. It is, perhaps, the biggest event that Lohara will ever witness. The names of the kings of Kashmira have always been evoked by the people with fearful respect but now one of them will be marrying their princess—and this has automatically elevated Lohara to a newfound status. Subsidiary kings and landlords have descended on Lohara to offer their help; relatives from near and far have begun to crowd the palace.

My mother is torn between joy in Udayaraja and grief at my impending departure. My father, meanwhile, seems to be in a permanent celebratory haze, often drink-induced, and there is very little governance in Lohara these days, for his ministers keep him company. I spend precious moments with Udayaraja, stroking his soft, white skin and smiling into his big, black eyes that are so like mine and my mother's. When I reflect on the fact that I will never see him take his first step or utter his first word, my heart fills with sadness. Will he remember me, I wonder. Will Didda just be a name to him rather than the memory of a real person? Will anyone ever tell him stories about me or describe to him what I look like right down to my lame foot?

'You must tell him everything you can about me,' I instruct Naravahana. For days now, I have been closing my mind to the impending separation from him, my oldest friend. Valga, at least, will stay with me—and I am intensely grateful for that—but the prospect of losing Naravahana is unbearable. I wonder miserably how I will manage without him by my side like a faithful shadow of my own self; without his constant chatter about his beloved horses that would always leave me mystified and amused; without his steady, unflinching, unwavering support. But this is my new life. I must step into it with faith in myself. I must cut all ties with my previous life, even if it means cutting away all comfort.

'I won't be here to tell him, princess,' he remarks drily.

I whirl around, surprised. 'Are you going back to Gandhara? Why don't you stay on here? You've made a place for yourself in the palace.'

'My place is with you, princess,' he says firmly. 'I will go with you to Kashmira.'

My heart leaps in delight but I turn my face away, so that he won't see how much this means to me. 'It will be hard for you,' I warn him. 'Everything will be unfamiliar and difficult in Kashmira.'

'As it will be for you,' he observes.

'But what about your father? What would he want you to do? Shouldn't you ask him?'

'I have already informed him of my decision,' he answers. 'He left me here in your service, so he knows I will follow you.'

'I thank you, then,' I say gravely. 'However, if you change your mind before we go, you should let me know. I will not think amiss of you.' I do not say aloud what both of us know: he will not change his mind; he will accompany me to my new home. His will be a dearly familiar face to me—as will Valga's—in a land of complete strangers. And all at once, I find myself viewing my future with a semblance of equanimity.

I see King Kshemagupta only on the day of our marriage and then not before the actual ceremony. I had heard his entourage ride in on the previous day, the horses' hooves thundering up towards the entrance to our palace. I had heard the songs of welcome being sung by our bards and several male voices raised in conversation but, to my disappointment, wasn't able to distinguish the actual words being exchanged.

Naravahana who could have brought me news is not allowed near the king and his companions. This is, clearly, the most important set of visitors to ever grace Lohara and hence, only the highest and ablest of the land must be allowed near the esteemed guests. Even Vigraha is banished from the scene and I see him sulking near his rooms.

I know that my father must be in a state of extreme anxiety. Kashmira, bigger and tremendously more powerful, can swallow us up in a simple battle if she so chooses. My father's obsequiousness towards Kshemagupta stems from this stark fact.

I have tried to block my future husband from my mind all this while but now, I finally allow myself to dwell on him, to speculate about his looks and personality, to wonder whether he will like me. Can it be that I will find happiness with him? Could the stories I have heard about him so far be untrue? Are they mere malicious rumours designed to wreck my peace of mind? If so, who has put them about? My father? Vigraha? Someone who is against this match? Or are they, in fact, true, unassailable fact?

The more I think, the more the puzzlement grows in my mind, till it assumes monstrous proportions. This is the worst dilemma I have ever faced in my life.

However, the morrow will reveal all—and I will have to face reality even if it is unpalatable.

VALGA

She looks beautiful as a bride, so beautiful that everyone gasps audibly when her veil is lifted. Her body is wrapped in the best silks and jewellery that money can buy and her face is glowing, impossibly radiant. The king of Kashmira looks pleased with her and how can he not? No one in the palace today can take their eyes off her. I feel a thrill of pride course through me. Who dares to taunt her with being a cripple today? Her regal bearing astounds even those of us who have known her in her most vulnerable moments.

I am by her side throughout the long and lavish ceremony. If King Simharaja intended to impress King Kshemagupta with his wealth, I think he has been eminently successful. A thousand servants have worked night and day to transform the palace into a paradise of rich tapestries and glowing lights and gleaming floors. The best cooks have been pressed into service and the guests from Kashmira are pampered with the choicest food, the most delectable sweetmeats. There is rich wine served by the prettiest women of Lohara to wash down the meals, while handsome stewards hover nearby, eager to fulfil the pettiest request. The bedchambers have been luxuriously furnished and decorated with the flowers of the season so that a floral aroma wafts through every corridor of the palace.

King Kshemagupta is charming, even handsome. He is continually surrounded by a coterie of companions who hang on his words and appear to worship him. He is not very tall and is fairly thin. His face, that is beginning to show the ravages caused by continual drinking, is marked by a bright orange beard, which, I am told, is the prerogative of the kings of Kashmira. They dye their beards with saffron and no one else is allowed to copy them on pain of death. His smile is arresting, though, and he bestows it freely. Even I am not immune to his charm and so, I have to constantly remind myself that he is a weak and dissolute man. Yet when his eyes alight on Didda, they fill with warmth and gentleness and I can allow myself the hope that he will treat her well, that this match might not be as doomed as it first appeared to be.

King Simharaja, meanwhile, is at his loquacious best. To observe his charming demeanour, one would be hard put to imagine him as the surly, bad-tempered, selfish person he actually is. He pretends to an affection for Didda that he has never ever felt and extols her virtues as if there is no end to his litany of praise for her.

The queen keeps to the background. Perhaps she does not trust her tongue or her temper when faced with her husband's duplicity. The little prince, Udayaraja, provides a handy excuse, in this regard. She gives the impression of being occupied with him at all times when it is, in fact, his specially-appointed maids and servants who are.

Didda is tired after the ceremony but we will have to leave as soon as we can to make it to Kashmira before nightfall. She leans against me heavily. I know that her bad foot is aching but only the quickening of her breath tells me so. I have already packed my few belongings and have supervised the packing of hers. I did not bring much with me when I came here and my years at Lohara have only added a few silk clothes to my old, well-worn ones—the bounty of the princess. My head does not get turned by wealth—it is not in my nature—but sometimes I run my fingers over the fine cloth and marvel at the fact that I own these at all.

My aunt is sorry to see me go, not because she has a fondness for me but because there will be no one to cook and clean and serve her when I am gone—chores that I had continued with whenever I had the time, even after I was elevated to Didda's service.

'I am a poor woman,' she tells me, her face screwed up in self-pity, 'yet I have taken care of you as if you were my own daughter.'

This is so grossly untrue that I am outraged but I don't want to get into a heated argument with this irascible woman on the very day that I step into yet another new life.

I take a last look around the squalid room that I had shared with her. 'I don't know if I will see you again,' I say, 'but I pray for god's blessings upon you.'

She does not bless me or wish me well but I would have been surprised if she had. I have tried to share my newfound wealth with her and look after her needs over my years in Lohara but have never heard a word of gratitude in return. I am relieved to be rid of her for she is an aching reminder to me about the family I have lost, my mother and siblings whom I will never see again.

Didda is quietly brave at the time of our departure. She bows before her parents; her father strokes her head in blessing but she flinches away slightly so that no one really notices and then folds herself in her mother's embrace. She takes her infant brother from his nurse's arms and kisses him on his brow. This is the only moment when I fear she will break down but she remains poised in her grief and turns her back on her home determinedly.

She sags against me for a brief moment but I steady her while helping her into the palanquin that is to carry her to her husband's home. She had the option to ride behind him but her dread of horses remains and she is content to remain unseen in the palanquin while she embarks on the journey that will leave her past behind.

Naravahana is among our main escort group and I see him shoulder aside the accompanying soldiers from Kashmira as if to indicate that he has a proprietary right on the palanquin and its occupants.

I settle her against the embroidered cushions within and ask if she would like something to eat or drink. I know she has taken very little by way of refreshment all this long day and so, she must be famished and exhausted. She drinks some water and consents to have a crumb of bread but no more than that.

'You must keep up your strength, princess,' I say firmly. 'It would look amiss to the people of Kashmira if you came upon them in a fainting condition.'

'Queen,' she corrects me and I bite my tongue. I can't take our old, easy familiarity for granted any more. She is an exalted royal personage now, higher in status than even her husband owing to the royal blood that has always run in her veins. I must show her the proper courtesy due to her rank.

'Forgive me, Queen Didda,' I murmur and then maintain a respectful silence. She does not break it all the way to Kashmira but stares out of the sides of the embroidered screen instead.

It is an interminable journey, or so it seems to me, as even my strong shoulders are beginning to droop with the strain. We have been confined to the palanquin for hours on end and I long to stretch my legs and walk a little to relieve the strain in my body. Although the sun has set a while ago and it is rapidly becoming more difficult to discern the landscape outside, I know that we have traversed deep, wooded jungles that we later learn are the Shimika—and then through a long valley that echoes with merry streams and the farewell cries of birds that are

beginning to roost in the trees. A fragrance fills the air—
it is indefinable and unfamiliar to me but I know that the
valley of Kashmira is renowned for its beautiful flowers
and plants, and that it rivals any other country in this
realm in the bounties of nature with which it is amply
blessed. I had thought Lohara to be much prettier than
Udabhanda but I am to learn that Kashmira is a paradise
on earth and simply breathtaking in its loveliness.

I must have dozed off, at some point, for I wake with a
jolt to hear raised voices and shouts around the palanquin.
Didda is awake and staring at the screen. I am dimly aware
that we have crossed a drawbridge and that our palanquin is
slowing down. More shouts punctuate the dark, aromatic
air and lights show themselves in bright blurs through our
screen. The neighing of horses and the creaking of their
saddles add to the sounds and then we are gently lowered
to the ground. Almost at once, the screen is thrust aside
by an impatient hand.

'Welcome to your new home, my queen,' says King
Kshemagupta. 'Welcome to Kashmira, to Shrinagara.'

Didda bows her head in gracious response and
allows me to lift her out of the palanquin and set her
on the ground. Her eyes are heavy with exhaustion, her
face pinched, but she gathers herself so well that pride
stabs through me all over again.

The air is sharp with a cold wind that stings us
through our layers of clothing. Before us looms the palace

that appears magnificent even in this dim light. I can see a line of people assembled by the steps, clearly waiting to welcome their king and his bride.

I hurry to support Didda as she prepares to follow the king, but the latter sets me aside and offers his arm to her instead. I stifle a prickle of resentment and prepare to follow the royal couple. Naravahana is by my side, trying to look confident, as I do too, but failing to conceal his apprehension. Perhaps he is wondering what his role will be in this new scheme of things. Will he be allowed to serve Didda or be sidelined by the Kashmiri guards? I find my tired mind filling with the same sort of worries. Will Didda or the king appoint someone else to execute my job, someone whose shoulders are stronger than mine? I shiver, partly from cold, partly from fear.

Didda, meanwhile, has reached the row of courtiers and ministers, all of whom are prostrating themselves before her and offering humble words of welcome. She smiles and nods, and holds on heavily to the king's arm. He stops first before a tall, elderly man with watchful eyes and a hooked nose that reminds me of an eagle's beak. He wears grander robes than anyone else here and wields an air of authority even though he is in the king's presence.

'This is Phalguna, my prime minister and father-in-law,' declares the king with a slightly craven air. The man bows low and then straightens, his eyes fixed on Didda.

I can sense rather than see her stiffen and can guess at the thoughts in her mind. This is the father of a rival and the one who has apparently taken over the power that should rightfully be in the king's hands. Didda's answering bow is perfunctory and the expression in her eyes inscrutable but I know—and she knows—that he has recognised an enemy.

The king then turns before a stocky man with a thick scar running down his cheek and arms as thick as pillars.

'This is Rakka, our commander-in-chief,' he tells Didda, 'and he has saved us many a time from those who envy our wealth and territories.'

He gestures next towards a fox-faced man. 'And this is Mahiman,' he says with real warmth in his voice. 'He is Phalguna's grandson, the son of another daughter. And this is Patala, another grandson and the son of yet another of his daughters.' A youth with a vapid face is ushered forward and he bows to Didda, as does Mahiman.

'Welcome to the court, Queen Didda,' says Mahiman smoothly. His smile is wolfish now. Is it my imagination or is he trying hard to conceal his hatred for her? His tone and manner are somewhat insolent, verging on the edge of expected propriety. Beside me, Naravahana draws a breath and I realise he has noticed it, too.

Didda passes on and acknowledges a few other courtiers. The line seems endless and I wonder how they expect her to remember all these names and faces when she is so obviously tired. At this point, she shivers slightly, drawing her thick travelling robe more closely around her.

The king clicks his tongue and looks remorseful. 'Forgive me, my queen!' he exclaims. 'You should not be out in this cold night air listening to me talk. There will be time enough for all that later. Come, let us go into the warmth.' And he draws her into the confines of the palace where a gaggle of maids immediately surrounds her, clucking in concern.

Naravahana and I follow, somewhat tentatively. As the huge, carved entrance door swallows us up, misery swamps my mind. Is it due to the long journey at the end of an otherwise exhausting day or to the fact that I am no longer needed?

LORE AND AN HEIR

DIDDA

I think he loves me. No, I am sure of it—there is no need for doubt, in this regard. When he looks at me, his face lights up as if from some radiance within. When he talks to me, his voice is low and full of concern. When he touches me, he is gentle and tender. He has ordered that no expense be spared for my clothes, my accessories, my amusements. He is solicitous to the point of being stifling. He wants to know where I go, what I do and to whom I speak. He wants to know if I am happy, if I am content with him for a husband.

But am I? I do not reciprocate his love—this much I am sure of. There are times when he disgusts me with his uncouth behaviour and rough talk. There are times when I despise him for listening so cravenly to Phalguna and the others. There are times when I am angered by his misplaced priorities, when he thinks that going on a jackal hunt is more important than convening a council of his ministers and formulating policy or attending to the grievances of his subjects.

If I could, I would rip all the flatterers and false men from him like I would a soiled hem from my dress. I would show him that they are preying on him and his riches, that they would see him dead without scruple if he were to stop squandering his wealth and attention on them. They call him *Kankanavarsha* , 'Rainer of bracelets', and I have actually seen them throw out their arms before him so that he can cover them in gold. At this rate, the treasury will be depleted and the kingdom brought to its knees. But does he care?

And yet, there has been a change in him since our marriage—or so I gather from stray remarks at court. Increasingly, he is spending more time with me and less on his frivolous pursuits of earlier years. His gambling mates are often turned away from his door; he is curt with his explanations; he is trying hard to alter his agenda. He seems to be fascinated by my talk, my questions, my observations—and I exert myself in trying to dazzle him, bewitch him. It seems I am succeeding, much to the chagrin of Phalguna, in particular, who had thought I would be relegated to the shadows soon after my wedding.

The court here is very different from the one at Lohara. It is larger and more complex, and comprises chiefs, ministers and officials of varied ranks. Of these, there are two powerful bodies that are often pitted against each other in the jockeying for royal favour—the Ekangas or bodyguards and the Tantrins or foot soldiers. In the past, or so Chandralekha tells me, they have been involved in the choice of royal candidates to the throne, in the functioning of the administration and in the deposition of rulers. Fall foul of them, she says, and they will discredit you or worse.

She and I are friends. I never meant for this to happen for I came to Kashmira regarding her as my prime rival and determined to oust her from the king's affections. As it happened, I needn't have bothered. Chandralekha is a mere pawn in the hands of her father and nephews. She is timid and mild, and seeks nothing more than to live her life in the shadows. She does not crave power or position; she only yearns for some affection. This, however, has been denied to her by fate. Her mother died while giving birth to her; her father, Phalguna, only sees her as a stepping stone to the throne; her nephews, Mahiman and Patala, pursue an agenda of their own that sometimes requires her intercession with the king. That the king favours her no more is not the point; she is duty-bound to further the interests of her power-hungry family whatever her feelings on the matter.

Now she clings to me for companionship and is eager to tell me whatever I need to know about my new home. It was she who told me about Vamana and Jishnu—the wandering dice-players who have found a place in the court and are loath to leave, prompting the king to gamble and encouraging him to mock the learned men at court who seek to restrain him—and about Hari and Dhurjati, experts in the art of procuring women for the king's pleasure, and coaxing him into jackal hunts in the nearby forests of Damodararanya, Lalyana and Shimika.

The most disturbing tales, though, are those she tells me of Parvagupta, my husband's father, who was descended from a family of writers and who served King Yashaskara of Kashmira as a clerk.

'He looted King Yashaskara of two and a half thousand gold pieces,' she says. 'And this was as the king was dying! He had hidden the money but Parvagupta found it and snatched it from him.'

'And then?' I breathe, hanging on her every word.

'Then he took over the king's property—and it was extensive, you know. He kept the lion's share for himself and distributed the rest among his cronies.'

'But who was the ruler then? Didn't King Yashaskara have a son to succeed him?'

'He did—a boy, Sangramadeva. But he was too young to rule. And Parvagupta had a dastardly plan in mind.'

I lean forward, transfixed by her tale. The rumours of Parvagupta that had reached my ears at Lohara had been vague, unformed, ambiguous—merely hinting at his ferocious ambition. Had the facts been deliberately kept from me?

'Parvagupta put Sangramadeva's grandmother on the throne as a puppet-regent,' Chandralekha goes on. 'The Ekangas were suspicious of his intentions but he allayed these by pretending to serve Sangramadeva diligently. This went on for a short while until one day, when there was a very heavy snowfall, Parvagupta surrounded the palace with his troops. The snow made it difficult for the palace guards to sound the alarm or muster the royal troops.'

'What happened then?' I ask, although my heart has told me the answer.

'Parvagupta seized the boy-king, Sangramadeva, and killed him. Then he hung a heavy stone around his neck and threw the body into the waters of the Vitasta where it sank without a trace. After that, Parvagupta became the sole ruler of Kashmira. Those who had opposed him earlier submitted to him for fear of his cruel reprisals. And, of course, he promptly dyed his beard saffron so that all should know he was the ruler.'

I nod. The sight of Kshemagupta's vivid saffron beard had surprised me at first until I was told that this was one of the marks of sovereignty in Kashmira.

'How did Parvagupta die?' I ask after a pause, my mind trying to grapple with the unsavoury details I have just heard.

Chandralekha shrugs her shoulders. 'For all that, he only ruled for two years and then he died—painfully, it seems—of dropsy. Some said it was inevitable due to his violent excesses. Others said it was a form of divine retribution.'

So I am married into a family of looters and murderers who do not possess a single drop of royal blood in their veins. Should I be I surprised, then, that this is a court filled with villains and fools, rotten to the core and a hotbed of vice besides? What am I doing in its midst? My husband's ancestry is one of clerks, scribes, lowly courtiers, while I—I am so high above them in blood and regality that I have brought lustre to their line. Yet the unfairness of the world decrees that I, as a woman, have abandoned my ancestry and adopted that of my husband. But I haven't, not inwardly. The world doesn't have to know that I still cling to my Lohara and Shahi connections, that I take pride in having descended from them.

I am already beginning to make my presence felt. My first skirmish with Phalguna has shown that I am a woman who will not easily follow the dictates of others but has a mind of her own. He thinks that as prime minister and the king's father-in-law, he has the right to command everyone in the realm and bend them to his will—and I am glad to have proved him wrong.

On the morning after my arrival in Kashmira, when I was still trying hard to get my bearings, he entered my ornate audience chamber, bowed and said curtly, 'The horses are ready for your escorts, Queen Didda. I will send two of my guards to guide them back to Lohara.'

I frowned. 'Which escorts do you speak of?'

'I believe their names are Valga and Naravahana,' he replied. 'You will have no more need of them here. Our own attendants will take on the work that they did for you in Lohara.'

My eyes flashed with anger and I rose to my feet, my hands clenched tight. 'Valga and Naravahana stay here,' I said, my voice shaking with fury. 'You will not make decisions on my behalf—not now, nor in the future.'

He bowed, his face devoid of expression. 'Forgive me. I will not make the same mistake again.'

When I think about the incident now, I realise it must have been his carefully-designed ploy to test my strength, to see how far he could push me. I hope he has his answer now. Valga remains by my side as always, and as for Naravahana, I have persuaded my husband to take him into his council. He has agreed because he is always eager to please me and now I have the satisfaction of seeing my dear friend occupied with administrative matters and impressing everyone with his sincerity—although he barely has the time to visit me due to his increased responsibilities. He misses his horses, I know, but Valga tells me he visits the stables at the end of each day to croon over the beasts and feeds them the apples that litter the royal orchard.

There are others who I need to be wary of right now. Rakka, the commander-in-chief, who is dour and uncommunicative; Yashodhara, Himmaka and Mukula, battle-hardened soldiers for whom Phalguna seems to nurture a special fondness; and, of course, Mahiman and Patala, who strut around the court, secure in their relationship with Phalguna, their grandfather, and potential troublemakers—or so it seems to me.

There is much for me to do here. I am trying to acquaint myself with the history and traditions of Kashmira, to familiarise myself with the landscape, particularly of Shrinagara. This capital city is an ancient one, lined by the magnificent River Vitasta; and girded by sparkling lakes, deep gorges and beautiful gardens that differ so starkly from the tough, hilly terrain of my childhood.

In fact, I am told that all of Kashmira was once a lake and later, the material form of Goddess Parvati. Chandralekha says that, therefore, any occupant of the throne of Kashmira is seen as a part of the goddess. This is, perhaps, why most people worship the Ardhanarishvara form of Lord Shiva—half-man, half-woman— in this valley. I find all these facts endlessly fascinating and accumulate them greedily like a squirrel hoarding nuts. Chandralekha teases me for my obsession with stories but they are a vital key to understanding a land and its people.

I am also getting to know Kshemagupta's subjects— and mine—as the days go by. They throng the area near the palace for a glimpse of me, and I nod and smile at them, delighting in the fact that they seem to approve. I am warned, however, that they are fickle, quick to switch loyalties, and in requirement of constant appeasement. At the moment, though, they look affable and enthusiastic, so I dismiss the warning as a mere exaggeration.

My husband, meanwhile, has taken it upon himself to show me the famous shrines that dot this land. Perhaps he thinks I am religious and that nothing would please me more. If I tell him that I have often been angry with god for making me a cripple, would he be shocked? Would he love me any less? But then I reflect that this is the man who stormed a Buddhist shrine and broke it down, building a temple from its ruins and using the wealth that he stole for his own purposes. Making shrines out of ill-gotten riches—as he is wont to do and his father was before him—does not gain one any virtue but how do I tell him this without offending him?

He takes me to the temple of Parvagupteshvara built by his father and I marvel at the beautifully carved idol of Lord Shiva enshrined within.

'My father was a very pious man,' he says and I nod, averting my eyes so that he can't read the expression in them.

We also visit the Sureshvari tirtha where Parvagupta is supposed to have breathed his last and I listen as my husband intones a prayer for his father's soul.

The temple to Shiva that my husband has built from the ruins of the Jayendravihara is the Kshemagaurishvara, sprawled across one of the streets of a city market. The people fall back respectfully as we approach and I hear shouts of 'Long live, Queen Didda' that thrill me to the core of my being. I smile at them, resolving to distribute clothes and food among the poor people later so that I secure their prayers and blessings.

All at once, I hear a different cry—*Diddakshema, Diddakshema!* The name is taken up on all sides so that the air eventually resounds with it. The shouts rise louder and louder so that this name that they have given us becomes a roar that penetrates the sky. Perhaps it can be heard all the way to the southwest in Lohara! I look around me and there is just this one word on everyone's lips.

'My people know how much I love you,' says my husband proudly. 'Look how they have conjoined our names to make one!'

I smile. This is power indeed.

VALGA

She is pregnant with her first child. She was suddenly, unexpectedly sick one morning, and the midwife confirmed what I was beginning to suspect. The king is celebrating as if the child is already born but it is clear to me that the joy is confined to him alone. I saw the prime minister, Phalguna's face fall in an unguarded moment when the news of the impending birth was announced in court. It seems he has plans of his own and his eyes—and those of his entire family—are on the throne. I try to warn the queen about this but she already knows.

'This court is dangerous, Valga,' she observes. 'No one is really as they seem.'

She says that we will wait to see what happens but her lips tighten and her face takes on the determined look that I have come to know and love, so I know that all will be well. I hope for her sake that it will be a boy but the king loves her so much that I think he will forgive her even if it is a girl. Only time will tell.

Meanwhile, I am trying to make myself so useful to her that no one dare send me away—as the prime minister had once attempted to do. I am there by her side at all times, offering my shoulder as support, lifting her over uneven ground, carrying her in my arms when she is tired, fetching everything that she needs. So, too, is Naravahana, although he is restricted by the demands at court and his manifold duties. I often see his face crease in concern as he looks at her and I feel an unfamiliar pang. Is it jealousy? Will he ever look at me that way? I turn away, confused, and try to make sense of my feelings. It seems that my thoughts about him have grown over the years into something else, something totally different. He has always been there by Didda's side, as I have been, and we have taken each other's presence for granted all this while, I suppose.

Yet, all of a sudden, I find my gaze lingering over his thick black hair; his fair, smooth skin; his honest brown eyes. My face feels hot and I turn away. My practical self comes to the fore shortly thereafter and rescues me from the mire of feelings I have fallen into. Naravahana worships Didda, this much I know. When she is around, he has eyes for no one else. It is as if he is dazzled by her radiance, entranced by her quick wit and completely in thrall to her presence. I need to recognise the bitter truth—he is hardly likely to notice my plain, heavy features and suddenly become attracted to me. No, I have to content myself with the fact that he views me as a friend, someone who shares his concern for his queen, someone who is a reliable presence by her side—as is he. Nothing more. And yet, in some strange way, even this much is enough.

Queen Didda's belly is growing bigger. Her beauty seems to bloom with every passing day and draws all eyes to her at court. The king fusses around her and has ordered that all her requests be fulfilled—be it to taste a particular type of food or to adorn her long hair with flowers that grow only on the higher mountain slopes. An army of servants has been detailed for her service but it is only to me she turns when she needs something—or to Naravahana if he is around.

I am with her when the king arrives, bearing a painted wooden box, which he thrusts into her hands. An air of mystery surrounds him.

'Open it,' he urges, and when she does, coins fall onto her lap, gleaming in their newly-minted brightness. She holds one up and I can see the proud inscription on its surface. *Diddakshema*, it proclaims, and she throws back her head and laughs in delight.

The king brushes the coins aside and takes her hand in his. 'I want our love to be known to all,' he says softly. 'You are my life, Didda, my world.'

She makes no reply but he doesn't seem to be waiting for one. Such is the extent of his fascination for her.

Abhimanyu is born on a cold winter's night. I am frozen despite standing as near to the fire as possible and bundling myself in every thick garment I possess. It has never been this cold in Lohara—or even in Udabhanda. The ground, the trees, the air itself is cloaked in a white sheet that seems to smother every single sign of life.

The brooding silence that reigns within and outside is terrifying to me.

I can't seem to stop shivering as I wait for the midwife to deliver the child that seems to be making its torturous way out of the queen. Several hours have passed since the beginning of her pains but Didda's screams have lapsed a long time ago into near-silence, and the midwife is chafing her hands and coaxing her to stay alert. If she lapses into unconsciousness, it could be serious for her and the child, so my heart is filled with dread and prayers spill from my lips in a continuous stream.

The child slips into the world on the lingering note of his mother's scream. The midwife clucks in satisfaction that it is a boy and gives him to the exhausted Didda to hold. Tears of relief and happiness fall down my cheeks as I bend over her and the child.

'You are crying, Valga.' Her tone is tired but accusing. 'This is a time for happiness, isn't it?' And she touches the baby's brow gently with a finger.

'My child,' she murmurs. 'My boy.'

I look closely at the baby who is mewling like a kitten and flailing his fists in indignation.

'His mother's temper?' I wonder. He has her straight nose and big eyes, as far as I can make out, at this point. This helpless child has a throne in his future and enemies to contend with that he doesn't even know. All at once, it seems too huge a burden to place on this tiny scrap of life and my heart swells with pity.

My duties increase after his birth for Didda does not trust anyone but me to carry him around. I can hardly feel his weight in my arms but I hold him as if he were a precious casket that would shatter and break with rough handling. The choice of name is hers but the king does not demur. His gratitude to her for giving him an heir is almost overwhelming to watch. His love for her has doubled, even trebled. She can ask for the sky and he will place it in her hands. At this moment, nothing else exists for him—his gambling companions, his hunting mates, his other wife. He is consumed by her and her alone.

Gifts come from Lohara to mark Abhimanyu's birth, along with a message from the queen's mother. She opens the letter eagerly and reads it aloud to me. Her mother sends her blessings and Udayaraja's love, and notes that Didda's grandfather, King Bhima Shahi, intends to visit her soon to see his great-grandson in person. Didda is ecstatic—she has always loved her grandfather—and immediately begins to supervise the preparation of a chamber for him and to devise plans for his entertainment during his stay.

'We must take him to the sacred springs of Martanda,' she declares. This has lately become one of her favourite haunts. She loves to sit on the grassy verge by the waters and gaze into their luminous depths. Later, she will pluck some wild flowers that grow in profusion near the springs and have me braid them into her long hair. All of Shrinagara is beautiful but this seems to be the loveliest spot of all. Its very air is bracing, its solitude calming, its flowers and trees refreshing to the eye.

'You can take him anywhere,' says the king. 'If he is dear to you, he is dear to me—and we will treat him with all the respect and love due to him.'

When he says this, Didda's face softens but it does not match the adoration of his gaze; it never does. Sometimes I wonder whether she loves him at all.

It is slightly more than a year before King Bhima Shahi is able to visit us. He has been occupied with unrest in his realm, and it has taken him all this while to quell it and establish peace in Udabhanda. Although the delay has disappointed Didda, it has been well worth the wait for he brings along a very special companion in his royal train. It is Udayaraja, Didda's younger brother, who is now able to walk on his own and is no longer a baby.

Didda snatches him up with a cry of delight and smothers him in a long embrace.

'I thought you would be happy to see him,' remarks her grandfather. 'His parents didn't want to part with him but I promised to take good care of their precious son.'

When he is released, at long last, from his sister's embrace, Udayaraja's look is solemn. 'Must I bow to you?' he asks gravely.

Didda laughs and ruffles his hair. 'No, you needn't bow to me now. But you might need to later—when you're grown up and you come to visit me.'

She is transformed by their visit. Her face radiates happiness and I see her laugh openly for the first time since we came to Kashmira. King Kshemagupta treats his guests with punctilious attention and orders that no expense be spared on their comfort during their stay—a fact that displeases Phalguna, whose attitude towards the visitors is one of barely-concealed hostility. He does not dare to voice his disapproval, though. In fact, such is the reputation of King Bhima Shahi that all the flatterers and parasites at court have vanished much like worms into the woodwork, leaving behind only those few who are sincere and honest.

King Bhima Shahi has kind words for both me and Naravahana. He praises us for looking after Didda all this while and requests us to continue doing so.

'For she is alone among sharks here,' he remarks astutely, 'and she will need her faithful friends around her as Abhimanyu grows older.'

I do not accompany Didda on the visit to the springs at Martanda for I am given charge of Abhimanyu for the day. He is a quiet child and no trouble at all but looking after any infant is hard work and I am on my toes throughout the day with no time for anything else.

This is perhaps why I only hear the startling news on the next morning when Naravahana accosts me near the throne room.

'Will the king be angry with her, do you think?' he asks worriedly.

I am puzzled. 'Why? What has she done?'

'King Bhima Shahi is building a temple to Lord Vishnu near the springs at Martanda; a mile north of them, actually. It's his decision—and hers. And it's to be called the Bhimakeshava temple after him.'

I am silent. If Naravahana's story is true, Phalguna and the others will be furious. This is, after all, only the adoptive country of Bhima Shahi's granddaughter, so how can he justify building a temple within it?

And yet, even as I pose this question to myself, an answer appears in my mind. He can do it for two reasons. The first is that he is powerful enough to do so.

The second and more important one is that his granddaughter's power is beginning to match his own.

LESSONS AND LOSSES

DIDDA

Life takes on an assured pace at the court of Kashmira. The days stream by and before I quite realise it, it is a decade since my marriage to Kshemagupta. Sometimes it seems to me that I have spent all my life here in Shrinagara. My earlier days at Lohara have begun to take on a dreamlike quality such that I often pause to remember details that remain frustratingly out of my mind's grasp. News from my mother continues to reach me—she writes frequently and in expansive detail. Udayaraja is a strapping young prince, popular everywhere he goes and the joy of his parents' lives. I suppress a pang of jealousy when I read this but it is slight and quickly gone. My brother has visited me only once or twice in these past years but each time, I have felt my love for him overwhelm me.

'Is he more important to you than I?' asks Abhimanyu, plucking at my sleeve and turning huge, hopeful eyes to my face. It is a strange feeling for him to have an uncle who is nearly as old as he is. They are playmates for the most part except for moments like these when doubt creeps into my son's mind.

'He is my brother.' My tone is serious, and he nods gravely.

'But I am your son,' he counters, and I smile inwardly at his sound logic, his argument that cannot be refuted.

'You are both precious to me,' I say finally. 'Each in his own way.'

He nods, content for the moment with this response.

Do I tell him that I used to spend hours gazing at his face when he was a baby, marvelling at the perfection of his fingers and toes, of his little nails that reflected my face, of his limbs, of every part of him? Do I tell him that when he took his first tentative step, my throat was choked with pride and emotion? Do I tell him that when he uttered his first sensible word that could be distinguished from his earlier babbling, I held his hands and nodded and smiled? Yet this is the natural reaction of all mothers anywhere in the world. Thus must my mother have watched over me and taken note of my first steps away from babyhood. And so,

I do not tell him anything. He knows that he is dear to me, but that I am not an indulgent mother who will fulfil his every whim. He must grow up to be someone worthwhile and I must watch over him carefully to ensure this.

I observe him sometimes when he is unaware of my scrutiny. There is a striking resemblance between us—in his eyes and nose and chin—but there is a quietude in him that neither his father nor I possess. I wonder whose qualities he has inherited. He is sweet-tempered and gentle, quick to emotion and unusually sensitive to the needs of others. It is almost as if he is a changeling—someone who has been passed off as my son—because he is so very different. And yet, it is this very difference that endears him to me, that makes me love him so fiercely. He is dear to his father, too, but even here I seem to eclipse Abhimanyu in his affection. I am everything to his father; he is but a part.

My dealings with the court are always abrasive, always fraught with tension, especially with Phalguna who has had to reconcile himself to the third place in the kingdom after the king and me. He treats me with courtesy but both of us know what is lurking beneath. And yet, he is a very capable administrator, one who smoothly covers over my husband's ineptitude in this regard, and I pay him grudging admiration for this. Hence, I do not bring his hostility to the attention of my husband, although he

75

would have been able to discern it if he were more astute and observant.

He is still fascinated by me but the novelty of the early years has worn off, so that he is slipping back into the clutches of his wastrel friends. He has let himself go to seed entirely and suffers from diseases related to obesity and a wild, undisciplined lifestyle. Yet he pays no heed to his physicians' warnings. He is often churlish with me on the few occasions when we are together. Even Abhimanyu holds little attraction for him now. If this is the life he wants to lead, then so be it. It matters less and less to me as time goes by.

Little by little, I am learning the intricacies of administration, the wheels behind the running of the kingdom. I persuade Naravahana to tell me about the matters that are deliberated upon by the council of ministers of which he is a part. He has inched his way to higher offices, impressing all by his sincerity and sagacity. He is now in charge of the accounts of the royal household and has also been told to keep an eye on two troublesome provinces to the western frontier of the kingdom. This is an exalted status indeed for an outsider who has been thrust upon the court, as it were, by me. Yet he remains the same in his reserve, his slight diffidence, his deference to me. And I am more grateful for this than I can say. He is the one constant factor in a world that shifts every minute to reveal new patterns. As is Valga.

News from home continues to reach me and I marvel at the reports of Udayaraja's newfound sagacity, his responsible conduct at the Lohara court.

'My grandfather might visit soon,' I tell Kshemagupta as I read one of my mother's missives. The sudden frown that shutters his face takes me by surprise.

'It seems as if he is more concerned about matters in Kashmira than his own court,' he remarks, a tangible sourness in his tone.

'He loves me,' I retort sharply. 'And his earlier visits have never bothered you.'

He is dressing up for a hunt and does not answer at once, intent on fixing the straps of his hunting jacket. Anger makes my breath rapid and I can feel my heart pounding against my chest. This is the work of his friends, perhaps Hari or Jishnu, or even perhaps Phalguna himself. They have altered his mind towards my grandfather whose presence at the Kashmira court always serves to reinforce my status. Lohara, of whom I am a hated representative, will always be lowly and insignificant to them.

My husband raises his head at last. 'I am going hunting,' he says, cravenly evading the tricky issue at hand. 'To the Damodararanya. More jackals have been sighted.'

He can see the distaste on my face and strokes my cheek with a gauntleted hand. 'You look beautiful when you're angry,' he murmurs. 'My jewel, Didda, we will honour your grandfather as always. Do not doubt that.'

My face relaxes into a smile. 'Must you go today? You are always with your friends these days. When do I get to savour your company?'

'This evening,' he says, drawing me close. 'After the hunt, I will come straight back to you.'

I watch him go, little knowing that his words will haunt me that night and for many nights thereafter. For he does come straight back to me—but unable to speak or move, wrapped in a thick shawl, a white discharge fouling his mouth, his body covered with eruptions. He is shaking uncontrollably and his skin is burning with fever.

'He fell ill almost as soon as we started hunting,' bemoans Hari, his face twisting into an expression that would pass for grief.

'We brought him back right away,' adds the rascally Jishnu. Both of them are clearly desperate to exonerate themselves of blame.

I ignore them and summon the court physician. He comes, his step slow, his face grave under his thick white brows. His pronouncement does not take long and my heart lurches with dread when I see his expression.

'It is the *luta* disease,' he says and I can hear the others hiss in fear. 'His end is upon him, Queen Didda.'

'He was in perfect health this morning,' I hear myself protest as if my words can reverse what has occurred; as if by pointing out the contradiction, everything would right itself.

'A man can be in perfect health in the morning and be dead of the *luta* disease by night,' he remarks drily. 'It catches a person unawares. There is no known cause and no known cure.'

A part of me is agitated, disbelieving, fearful of what has transpired. The other, more dominant part is assessing the situation, planning the next step, pondering ways to handle the aftermath.

The rest of the ministers have gathered by now, shock and dismay writ large on their faces. Not on all of them, though. Phalguna's face is wooden, that of Mahiman's is of tightly-controlled relief. His cousin, Patala, mirrors his expression. I notice all this without appearing to do so and my mind begins to grapple with ways to foresee what these enemies of mine will do. Will they kill Abhimanyu and take over the throne? Will they kill me because I am his mother and likely to defend his rights?

Naravahana is by my side, as unobtrusive as always. I beckon him closer.

'Get Abhimanya to safety,' I whisper. 'Then come back here to me.'

He nods and is instantly gone. I feel Valga's restless twitching behind me. 'Go with him,' I say softly. 'Keep my son safe.'

Then I turn my attention to the others. Phalguna steps forward and bows, and in my fevered imagination, I see the gesture as a purely mocking one.

'I have given orders that the king be made comfortable in his rooms,' he tells me. 'This is all we can do for him in his condition.'

'No,' I say firmly and his head snaps up in surprise. I have everyone's attention now. 'I want him to be taken to the Kshemamatha so that he can die in holy environs. He built it and now it is only right that he takes his last breath there.'

'But the matha is close to Hushkapura, a half day's journey from here,' Phalguna expostulates. 'It is in Varahakshetra, Queen Didda!'

'I know this kingdom as well as you!' I snap. 'Do not presume to tell me what I should or should not do. We can reach Varahakshetra in just a few hours if we ride fast. Put the king in the royal carriage. I will travel with him—and you will all follow me.'

In no time at all, we are on our way. It is clear that Kshemagupta is dying. He is unconscious now and barely breathing. His face is scarcely discernable under the rashes, his hair stiff with sweat. I sit beside him along with a distraught Chandralekha and two of my attendants as the carriage is swiftly borne away by the horses in the gathering darkness. Chandralekha gathers her silk robes more closely around her and stares at the king, speechless with grief. I have nothing to say to her, no words of reassurance or comfort.

I try and fill my mind with other thoughts in the vain hope of being distracted but to no avail. It will be winter soon and already the wind is sharp and unforgiving, blowing through the carriage despite the lowered screens and causing my maids to shiver. I am barely conscious of it as I look at the king, the man I have lived with for so many years, and try not to think of losing him. I have never loved him, this much I know. Yet my feelings for him have steadied into affection, a desired companionship. I will miss his endearments, his loving gestures, his flippant talk. I will miss the way he looked at me. His absence will leave a hole in my life.

And yet, I know that I will survive his loss. I will move on, grieved at having lost a friend but stronger for having known him, for having been cherished, for getting to know my strengths in an alien place. Alien no longer, this land has enveloped me in its beauty, in its starkness, in its radiance, and I know that I will not leave it to return to Lohara. My future is tied to Kashmira now and this is where my destiny will unfold. This is where I shall stay.

VALGA

I fear for her while we are away.

I tell Naravahana that we should hasten but he brushes my concerns aside, making sure that the prince is comfortable in the disused stables where we have taken him. This block of dilapidated rooms on the fringes of the former palace, an hour's ride from the present one, should be the last place that anyone would think of searching, so he will be safe for the time being. The prince is terrified but is trying hard to be brave and does not allow a single word of complaint at the rank interiors and filthy, straw-strewn floor to escape his lips. I find myself trembling with anxiety, my heart beating at twice its usual pace. Is the queen being paranoid or would someone actually try to kill him?

Naravahana posts one of his trusted servants near the stables at a vantage position atop a hillock from where he can view everything, yet remain concealed. Then we hurry back to our horses where they are peacefully cropping the grass and ride as fast as we can to Varahakshetra. My heart pounds faster. My horse races beside Naravahana's and I see his brow tensed with anxiety, his face pale. Now and then, he throws a glance over his shoulder to see if I am holding on but he is clearly relieved that I am able to match his pace. We ride on and on for hours, never stopping for a break or refreshment, although I am half-dead with fatigue.

When we enter Varahakshetra, at long last, the last rays of the autumn sun are painting the sky a vivid violet and then the colours merge, becoming indistinct, and everything around me blurs and grays in the night sky that has covered us. We hear the cries and laments from a distance and even before we dismount and walk into the Kshemamatha, we know that it is over. The king is dead. And the world has changed in a single day.

We find Didda in a chamber that has been hastily screened off as an enclosure, the entrance hung with the saffron cloth used by the matha's inmates. I hastily avert my eyes from the king's body that lies in the central passage, the priests forming a chanting cordon around it, the smoke from the fire stinging my eyes and hurting my throat. His body has decomposed rapidly; it will not stand the journey back to Shrinagara.

They are preparing a pyre to burn him and even then I do not see, I do not realise what is to happen. Instead, I look at Didda's wan face, her exhausted figure that droops slightly as it does when her lame foot aches more than usual. Yet when Phalguna enters the chamber almost on our heels, I see her straighten her back and look as regal as always—and my heart lifts with pride at her effort as I walk across to stand by her side.

'It is almost time,' he says, a curious mixture of pity and triumph on his face.

All at once, a figure stirs in a gloomy corner of the chamber and I recoil in fright. I have not noticed it before and I peer sharply at it now as it stumbles into the light. The face is disfigured with weeping, the limbs seem on the point of collapse—but I can discern that it is Chandralekha before us, her swollen eyes now alight with determination, her hand stretched towards her father. He bows and then embraces her, his expression as wooden as always, and then he looks at Didda.

'No!' Naravahana's voice slices through the dark air and it is then, only then, that what is to happen is borne home to me, crushing me with its horror. My Didda is to die. She will have to mount the funeral pyre with the king and burn to death in the flames that consume his lifeless body. My lips move in soundless protest and I clutch her arm tightly, my heart sinking. She looks at me and strokes my hand; she knows what is to follow. Yet her face is strangely serene below the obvious signs of grief that mark her—the faint line of tears that have coursed a line down her cheeks; her red, strained eyes.

'Queen Didda cannot die,' Naravahana says firmly and even through my dread, I feel a glow of admiration for his courage at this point. His face is shadowed but I can feel the tension emanating from him. It is the same as mine.

Phalguna turns to him and in this half-light, he looks evil, malevolent. 'It is the custom,' he says softly but his voice fills the room. 'She has no choice but to become a *sati*, a loyal companion to the king in death.'

Didda remains silent, her eyes fixed on them. I tighten my hold on her arm as if I will not let her go. And I won't, not ever—they will have to fight me to get to her and I know how to use the great strength in my limbs. I steal a glance at Chandralekha who waits by the entrance, unsure, apprehensive.

Naravahana suddenly changes his stance and kneels before Didda. 'You have a young son, Queen Didda,' he says. 'How can you kill yourself while he continues to live? How can you deprive him of both parents? How can ... ?'

'Where is the prince?' interrupts Phalguna, his gaze attentive. 'My servants say he is not in the palace. He should be here to pay his respects to his father, the king.'

'He is safe.' Didda's voice resounds, like Phalguna's, all over the room and I am struck by its confident, steady tone. 'And I will bring him before the court when his safety is ensured. Not before that.'

A sudden shadow of disappointment flickers across Phalguna's face but it is gone in the same instant as it appears.

'There are precedents,' continues Naravahana, now rising to his feet and addressing Phalguna, 'in literature and in our tradition. Instances when women have not become *satis* because of a higher purpose.'

'Which is this "higher purpose"?' barks Phalguna. I am filled with pity for his daughter who will be shortly dragged to her death by her remorseless father, someone who sees nothing wrong in this hateful custom and will consign her to the flames without a second thought.

'That of regency,' retorts Naravahana, seemingly gaining strength with every moment. 'That of fulfilling a mother's role, that of being a natural guardian.'

'There are others who can see to that,' persists Phalguna. 'We will look after the prince until he comes of age.'

'Let her be, father.' It is a shock to all of us to hear Chandralekha speak, to have her quiet voice take its turn in the cacophony of tones in the chamber. Phalguna takes a step back as if he has suddenly remembered her presence. 'Spare her life,' she continues. 'She has a son to live for, she has everything.'

'And you?' Didda breathes. 'What about *your* life?'

'I have nothing,' says Chandralekha simply. 'No husband, no child, no family to weep tears for me when I am gone.' At this last, Phalguna flinches but she goes on. 'You are a strong, courageous, noble woman,' she tells Didda. 'Don't waste your life in the flames. I will take your place.'

I see the glint of tears in Didda's eyes, her features soften in gratitude and affection. I have rarely seen this look on her face and Chandralekha seems to bask momentarily in its warmth.

Didda turns to Phalguna. 'I will not burn myself on my husband's pyre,' she says firmly. 'I will rule Kashmira in the name of my son. Understand this, Phalguna.'

He understands, only too well. For the first time, we see naked rage on his face. A rage that is fed when Kshemagupta's two wives embrace each other; seeming to draw courage, each from the other, to face their respective fates.

When the fire consumes the city, some days later, it is as if it consumes Didda's fortitude with it. It has been an exacting journey for her since the king's death. There are many at court who suspect her motives, many who denounce her for being a woman and yet ruling as regent. Abhimanyu is king only in name; it is his mother who takes all the decisions, who oversees the realm of Kashmira.

Meanwhile, Phalguna has disappeared and no one knows where he has gone. He vanished overnight with his loyal followers; some say he is in Parnotsa, where he has been sighted; others that he is in Varahakshetra. The royal spies are clueless and his grandsons, Mahiman and Patala, pretend to be.

Discontent simmers at court and it seems to me that Rakka, the commander-in-chief, is actively fostering them. He is everywhere at once, the livid scar that tears his cheek seeming to threaten those who would oppose him. He is positively thriving in Phalguna's absence. It was he, after all, who put it into Didda's head that the prime minister was planning to usurp the kingdom. Perhaps this was the reason behind Phalguna's disappearance.

It seems to me that Didda's reliance on Rakka is questionable and that his fleshy body is out to garner more wealth to adorn it, more posts to elevate it. He has already been made commander of the gates by her, a post that Phalguna previously held. His cronies are everywhere, mocking Phalguna's few remaining adherents, flaunting their leader's nearness to Didda. Perhaps she cleaves to him because of his superior knowledge of political wrangling or because she does not want to feel isolated at court.

The atmosphere is rife with rumours and predictions, with money openly changing hands between people in this uncertain political climate. Hardly anyone expects Abhimanyu to continue as king and there are even stories of neighbouring kingdoms eyeing the coveted throne of Kashmira. Consequently, I distrust almost everyone these days, except, of course, for Naravahana and the few who are loyal to him. He is now an important figure, second only to Rakka in status and someone who is respected by all. It is he whom Rakka hates most for he recognises an enemy in him, someone who will be an obstacle in his climb to power. Yet he does not dare oppose him for he is closest to the queen.

We are woken, that dreadful night, by the smoke that stultifies the city and which has been gathering in huge, noxious clouds for several hours. It has consumed the main markets and destroyed the ancient shrine of Vardhanasvamin in the centre of the city. Even as we attempt to make sense of what is happening, we can hear the dull roar of fire-ravaged buildings crumbling onto the street and crushing the people under the weight of their debris.

Didda, for once, is slow to react, lulled by Rakka's incomplete reports that conceal the actual extent of damage. By the time the townspeople batter down the doors of the palace in a desperate plea for help, and Naravahana orders that the city and palace be doused in gallons of water, the damage has been done. The once-magnificent Shrinagara is wrecked, a skeleton of ash and smoke and dead bodies. Mahiman and Patala are quick to foist the blame on the queen, calling her inept and incapable. Didda, in her confusion, relies more and more on Rakka and his patently false commitments.

It is Naravahana who establishes order in the city, who rides out with his followers to clear the ruins, and help the people to salvage their lives from the shambles of their surroundings and start afresh. It is he who persuades Didda to distribute money from the royal coffers to where it is most needed. It is he who reassures and soothes the tempers of the agitated populace.

It is, again, Naravahana, who demands an audience with the queen a week later, while she is with Rakka and his cronies, to announce that Phalguna has re-emerged and is marching with a large armed force to the gates of the palace.

'We must stop him and kill him,' insists Rakka.

'No, Queen Didda, you must placate him,' advises Naravahana, ignoring Rakka entirely and looking earnestly at the queen. 'He is a good administrator and the people trust him. At this stage, you cannot afford to antagonise him. For all you know, the reports of him trying to usurp the kingdom might have been false.'

The dull flush on Rakka's florid cheeks tells Naravahana that his words have struck home.

When Phalguna arrives with his massive band of followers, a short while later, Didda prepares herself to speak but it is Phalguna who advances and places his sword at her feet.

'Forgive me, O queen,' he murmurs. 'I feared those who were poisoning your ears against me. And so, I fled.'

'Do not desert me again,' says Didda and I rejoice that she has heeded Naravahana's advice. 'We have both made mistakes,' she adds, 'but we must look to the future and rule this land together to honour the memory of my husband, your former king.'

It is, if truth be spoken, a bargain with an enemy. Yet Didda has no other choice, at this point. She needs his support—and that of everyone else—till she is strong enough. Till she is able to shake them off and rule in her own right.

Till she is able to fulfil her destiny.

REBELLION AND BETRAYAL

DIDDA

It is time for me to step back and take a look at my achievements and failures since becoming regent for Abhimanyu. He is quiet and somewhat quiescent, and does not question my decisions. Perhaps he has no desire to be king and I wonder why the mere thought sends a flash of excitement through me. I should be worried instead! What will he do when I am gone? What if Phalguna hatches a plan to get rid of me—and I have no doubt he does that daily, even hourly? What then? Will my son relinquish the throne to those who seek it? Will he remain submissive and meek to the end of his days?

I try to shake some sense into him. 'Stand up straighter,' I command. 'A hunched posture does not suit a king.'

He sighs and I know that the restrictions that hedge his life right now are wearing him down. He cannot take a step without his guards leaping to his aid. He cannot see whom he likes or talk how he pleases for he is followed closely at every instant. He cannot even taste his own food unless someone checks it for poison. He cannot retire from the throne to lie down when his back aches or when he is tired. He cannot even determine when or how long he will sleep at night for there are set patterns to follow and his attendants must rouse him at a particular hour everyday so that the rituals of the morning may begin on time.

It is not easy being a king—yet how could he not revel in the idea of power that comes with it? At present, it is in my hands but he will exercise it himself some day. Why does it not thrill him to mount the throne? Why does he look so dull when he inspects his army? Why are his responses to his ministers so lacklustre?

A plan has been fomenting in my mind and I execute it before caution disables me. The fire and its aftermath, as well as the public skirmish with Phalguna, have shown me that I am on very shaky ground. I cannot muster any real support and there are a mere handful of those who are loyal to me. The people of Kashmira are a proud lot, particularly those of Shrinagara, who are conscious of belonging to a power centre. They loved me as Kshemagupta's wife; they regard me with suspicion as a regent. They chafe under the rule of one who does not fully belong to their land. They would rather trust a known devil, like Phalguna, perhaps, than an unfamiliar one.

Accordingly, for the next few months, I set out to know and understand those who I rule and command in Abhimanyu's name. I invite the ministers of my court, in turn, for a meal or for refreshments and get them to talk—about themselves, their families, their concerns, their joys. Most of them do, the others capitulate with some systematic prodding. Little by little, like trying to cross a very deep ocean a few spans at a time, I acquaint myself with all those who live or work in the palace— officers, courtiers, scribes, bards, musicians, guards, attendants, maids, servants—until there comes a time when I can call them by name and identify their kin.

'You have a prodigious memory, Queen Didda,' remarks Naravahana who knows what I am trying to do and is impressed when I call for the cook by name to praise a particular dish.

I laugh. 'Well, my teacher in Lohara always said that I was bright. You know that much. Brighter than Vigraha, anyway!' My face clouds now at the mention of his name.

A few days ago, I received an urgent missive from my mother informing me that my father has been ill for a while and that Vigraharaja has been openly talking of succeeding him to the throne of Lohara when he dies. My anger at his presumption almost made me call out my forces and dispatch them to Lohara but it was Naravahana who dissuaded me and made me see the folly in this.

'Vigraharaja hasn't done anything yet,' he pointed out.

'But who will protect my family from his ambition? Who will be Udayaraja's safeguard?'

'Your grandfather, King Bhima Shahi, will also be watching the situation. And he can reach Lohara faster than us.'

I subsided, calmed as always by his sound reasoning. I still fret about my brother but I can't do anything other than wait for more news.

Meanwhile, I reflect on whether my plan has succeeded—and I think it has. I am greeted by willing smiles and deep respect everywhere I go, and those in the palace, at least, are definitely warming to me, much to the dismay of Mahiman and his ilk. They are looking for a chance to usurp the throne but I am widening my support base, and popularity and goodwill are often more potent weapons than swords and arrows.

I now turn my attention to the people, my—or rather Abhimanyu's—subjects. I go on processions with him around Shrinagara and exert myself to be as charming as possible. I step down from the royal carriage at intervals

95

to inquire after an elderly citizen or to caress the cheek of an infant in someone's arms. I listen carefully to the people's complaints and instruct my attendants to attend to them. I visit the temples that my husband and other rulers have built in and around the city, and address the crowds gathered within.

'Pray for King Kshemagupta's soul,' I tell them. 'Pray for his son, the prince.'

Yet they cry, 'Long live Queen Didda!'

'It is as if *you* are the king,' observes Abhimanyu quietly.

I do not respond because he is right. Once again, excitement courses through me—a flare, quickly gone, but fierce while it lasts.

Trouble flares with Phalguna all over again. This time, it is over his grandson, Mahiman's behaviour and I summon the arrogant youth to question him. He has flouted my order to move to a distant province on the eastern border of Kashmira where I had thought to send him so that he does not foment trouble here. For too long now, I have seen him lurking about the court with his cousin, Patala, and a group of cronies who seem to dote on his every word and take their cue in disobedience from him. They mock me for being a woman and do not accept my rule but are careful not to be too obvious. Mahiman, however, has been skirting the edges of acceptable behaviour and does not even hide the sneer on his face when he looks at me.

He stands before me now, stiff, outraged, surly, only held in check by Phalguna's warning look.

'Why have you disobeyed my order?' I demand, without preamble. 'Why are you still here at court?'

Two eyes, full of venom, are turned on me and I can almost feel them sear my skin. 'This is my home,' he says, almost spitting out the words. 'I grew up here in this palace. King Kshemagupta treated me like his son.'

'He is dead,' I retort, 'and you now have a duty to fulfil.'

'I have no desire to be banished,' he says firmly and I hear Phalguna sigh, softly, exasperatedly.

'The king has ordered you to go,' I snap. 'And you will obey him on pain of death.'

He does not bow or respond but stares at me instead and my anger roars to life at his insolent, disrespectful gaze. Phalguna steps forward and motions to him to go. Mahiman barely lowers his head in deference to me and then strides out of my presence chamber.

'You will see to it that he obeys me,' I tell Phalguna sharply.

He inclines his head but does not say a word. His eyes are dark, watchful. He might have agreed to be on my side but I know that his heart is not committed to me. In his mind, I am a usurper of sorts, an unnatural woman who did not die alongside her husband but chose to play a part in the real world, the world of men.

Over the next few days, rumours of a disturbing sort reach me—that Mahiman is hiding in his father-in-law, Shaktisena's house, pretending to be ill; that Patala has joined him in his refuge; that they, in turn, have been joined by their friends, Himmaka, Mukula and Udayagupta—all hardened soldiers; and that others who claim to be disaffected have swelled their ranks. Names are bandied about: Eramantaka from Parihasapura, Udayagupta and Yashodhara from Lalitapura, and several others besides.

I summon Phalguna but he denies knowledge of any of this, of any conspiracy in the making.

'These are high-spirited youths, Queen Didda,' he observes. 'Once the heat in their blood has cooled, they will realise their folly.'

'And when will that be?' I retort.

He shrugs but I know the answer as well as he does. Mahiman and his treacherous band of rebels will not be satisfied until they have driven me and my son from the kingdom, until their common-blooded bodies have soiled the throne of Kashmira by their touch. I want to round them up and have them beheaded but Naravahana advises me to wait.

'They have not yet come out in the open,' he says gravely. 'If you act in haste, you will be accused of unfairness.'

So I grit my teeth in chagrin and wait. Summer is upon us but the nights often tremble in chilly winds, reminding us that this is a temporary phase, that winter will soon claim our land for itself. The palace orchard shimmers with blue crocuses, a shade akin to that of the Vitasta; the trees are heavy with apricots and almonds; the gardens are ablaze with flowers of every hue and every fragrance—but I have no eye for this loveliness. All I see before me is the ugliness of treachery, the rank smell of betrayal.

I wait for the enemy to show his hand but he is perhaps waiting for me to do the same—or to lull me into a sense of complacency with each passing day of inaction.

I am at the temple of Padmasvamin to the north of the palace with Abhimanyu. It is the anniversary of his birth and he always seems happier with religious quietude rather than an elaborate event and so, I have deferred to his wishes and brought him here. Naravahana is with us, along with our usual entourage. I have left a substantial force behind to guard the palace but I am on edge. All is serene in the temple precinct and yet, every sound seems magnified, each word seems like a shout.

99

I have always prided myself on my alertness but it is Naravahana who senses the danger before it descends on us. I turn in horror towards the dreaded sound—that of the steady tramp of horses along with the hoarse battlecries of a force on the march. It is not ours and I see Abhimanyu's face pale in realisation. They are coming for me, for us, and I am momentarily rooted to the spot with fear.

I see figures running towards the temple wall and vaulting over and I know with a cold certainty that our entourage has deserted us and that I am alone with my son; my porter-woman, Valga; my faithful Naravahana and one of his servants. The chief priest hurries out from the inner sanctum, his face ashen. If there is to be carnage within the temple enclosure, then his life might well be forfeit.

Naravahana seizes Abhimanyu by the hand. 'We must send him to the Shuramatha,' he cries and I nod, my mind coldly beginning to consider ways out of this predicament. The Shuramatha is close to the palace and guarded by the most stringent religious sanctions. None who seek refuge within its looming walls can be dishonoured or betrayed. My son will be safe with the priests and religious apprentices who live there.

'Lead us to your rear exit,' Naravahana orders the chief priest and he nods and hurries back inside, the others on his heels.

I turn to face the temple's main entrance, Valga by my side. Within minutes, Naravahana rejoins us. Now that Abhimanyu is in the capable hands of Naravahana's servant, heading towards safety, I do not waste my worries on him but focus, instead, on the crowd arrayed outside the temple's high gate.

It has fallen silent now but it is the hush that descends before decisive action. All the men are armed and I fleetingly wonder how Mahiman and Patala managed to raise the money for so many weapons. Clearly, this rebellion has been in the making for a long time and it must have the backing of several important people at court.

There are four men in saffron attire right at the front and I can see Mahiman's surly visage beside them. These must be the brahmanas from Lalitapura that Yashodhara is rumoured to have brought with him—impoverished, apparently, and looking for a way to augment their earnings. These men, the acknowledged leaders of many districts, would have been invaluable in creating religious frenzy and gathering adherents to the rebel cause. They can be fearsome in their zeal, ferocious in their commitment.

Nevertheless, a wry smile spreads across my face. I know how to deal with them; I know what gold from the treasury will mean to these mercenaries.

I touch Naravahana's arm and he turns to me. 'Tell them I want to negotiate,' I murmur. 'If they give us safe passage to the palace, I will make them rich beyond their wildest dreams. Tell them that.'

He smiles, knowing instantly who I mean and what I propose to do. I allow myself a fleeting stab of affection for him, this cherished friend and supporter of mine who can read my thoughts so easily.

And then I turn to face my enemies.

VALGA

She kills. Without scruple. Without compunction. Mahiman and Patala are slain on her orders and their bodies, weighted with stones, thrown into the Vitasta. Their cronies are rounded up and tortured to reveal all those involved in the plot and then they are impaled on swords. Their bodies are left on the garbage heaps outside the city for dogs and jackals to rip apart. Each and every member of the rebel force is executed. Their bodies share the same fate as that of Mahiman's cronies so that the city stinks of rotted flesh for days on end.

The brahmanas from Lalitapura have long disappeared with their stashes of gold. I worry, though, that their placation is temporary and they will return for more. Yet, for the moment, she has stepped, surefooted, over the ocean of her enemies, despite being a cripple.

One person is spared from the bloodbath— Yashodhara, the man from Lalitapura, whose reputation as a fierce warrior preceded him to Shrinagara. He is made the commander-in-chief of the army.

'How can you trust him?' I venture to ask her. 'He rebelled against you, after all! What if he fills the army with malcontents like him and eventually turns on us?'

She looks at me, amused. 'You understand very little of manipulation. Yashodhara is beholden to me now. I have broken the back of the rebellion and now he owes his life to me.'

'But what of Rakka?' I ask, troubled. 'You have taken his post away from him. Won't he resent it?'

'Leave that to me,' she says quietly. 'Your work is to support me with your strong arms. I will deal with the rest.'

A few days later, Phalguna—now a more silent, chastened version of himself—leaves the court, ostensibly on a pilgrimage to Parnotsa where his son, Kardamaraja, lives. He is accompanied by a handful of attendants and he departs without ceremony, unobtrusively. I reflect on how the wheel has turned, on his fall into disgrace owing to his family's machinations.

Rakka is made the prime minister and keeper of the gates in Phalguna's stead. He bows low before Didda and from where I stand beside her, I can see the flash of triumph in his eyes, glee writ large all over his scarred, wily face. The pronouncement has not gone down well with the rest of the court. Rakka was never a popular figure, and is known for his avarice and shirking of work. On the other hand, Phalguna, despite his ambitions and that of his family, was a capable administrator who had governed Kashmira capably in King Kshemagupta's time. How can such a one as Rakka step into the shoes of a giant?

'Your majesty might have made a mistake,' Naravahana tells her later. We are walking in the garden and although dusk is fast covering the land in her dark robes, I can still make out the vivid blues and pinks and yellows and reds of the flowers that surround us. Birds sing drowsily from the trees where they have come home to rest. I can hear the sharp commands of the palace keeper to the maids to hasten with lighting the lanterns that are to illuminate our path.

The twilight air is tranquil, peaceful, but Didda's sudden intake of breath tells me that she is angry. Increasingly now, she does not like to be questioned, for anyone to fault her judgement, for anyone to criticise her governance. I look at her and despite my apprehension, note how her fury makes her even more beautiful. Her eyes gleam, her nostrils are drawn in and her cheeks are flushed.

'Tell me,' she snaps. 'What is it that I have done now?'

'Rakka does not deserve the post of prime minister,' Naravahana responds, his face set in determined lines. If it were anyone but him, she would have cut them to size with her words—but he has always been her greatest support and so, however unwilling she is, she must hear him out.

'Do you think I decided this in haste?' she demands.

'No, Queen Didda.'

'Then why do you question me? Do you think I have no sense, no brains?'

'Forgive me ...'

'Just tell me what you want to say.' Didda sounds weary and she leans against me heavily. I broaden my shoulders and easily support her fragile weight with my arms.

'Should I carry you to the bench, Queen Didda?' I ask anxiously.

She shakes her head and turns to Naravahana.

'Rakka is untrustworthy,' he says quickly. 'He is greedy for power and will use his position for this. He will ...'

'It is either him or Phalguna,' she breaks in. 'Who else is there to choose from? Who else has so much experience? And I need someone whom the people will readily accept.'

'But ...'

'I will keep an eye on him,' she breaks in firmly. 'And so will you, my dear friend. Together we will foil his plans, if any.'

She ignores me, does not include me in this statement, and I feel momentarily bitter but then my mind quickly empties itself of rancour. Unlike them, I am always in the background, invisible, on the periphery of everyone's attention, so how would I expect to intervene in plots and make a difference? I am, after all, Didda's crutch, her physical aid. But then I, too, can keep my eyes and ears open and learn things that people often let slip in careless moments. Perhaps I will be able to overhear something vital, a fact that will ensure Didda's safety and that of her realm.

Naravahana suddenly turns to me and smiles as if he has read my thoughts. I smile back and nod my head. I am there for him, too, as much as I am for her.

Night has finally fallen and our faces are indistinct in the gloom. The lights have been lit all over the palace and its bulk looms over us, doubly huge and intimidating in the dark. Instinctively, I huddle closer to the others as a chill—borne of fear, not of the wind—creeps over me. It feels as if this land and its people are bearing down on the three of us, strangers from another place who have adopted this realm and are, perhaps, the only ones in it to genuinely care for each other. If any of us were to die tomorrow, I do not think a single tear would be shed by the people or a single heart throb in grief. Such is our fate. And her destiny.

I notice, in the days that follow, that Rakka has acquired a new follower at court—a thin, young man who walks behind him, carrying his quills and paper, and frequently assisting him in taking notes. I wonder whether he is a scribe but then dismiss him from my mind altogether because there are more important things to consider. Abhimanyu's impending wedding, for instance. It appears to be an ideal bond for he is shy, scholarly and timid, and she is meek and mild. Her name is Jayalakshmi, she is pretty but not obviously so, and she is clearly terrified of the queen.

Didda has chosen well, for Jayalakshmi's father, now deceased, had belonged to one of the old and wealthy royal families of Kashmira and, after the marriage, both his riches and his supporters will belong to Abhimanyu. Moreover, there is no likelihood of trouble from any quarter, least of all from Jayalakshmi's mild-mannered mother who, like her daughter, is completely in awe of Didda.

We are in the midst of the wedding preparations when Rakka approaches Didda with his young assistant by his side.

'Your majesty, I would like to introduce this talented youth to you,' he says, nudging the man forward. 'His name is Sindhu and he has a wonderful ability with numbers and figures. Indeed, I would even call him a magician, in this regard.'

Sindhu bows low and then turns adoring eyes on Didda. He is so obviously smitten by her looks and her regality that he can barely answer her questions. She asks him where he is from, what his family background is and what his qualifications are. The details he provides seem to me to be somewhat ambiguous and I wonder what Rakka hopes to gain by this introduction. In the next instant, it becomes clear—Rakka wants Sindhu to help him with the work of the treasury and is seeking the queen's permission for this. She gives it readily but I see Naravahana frown and I know that he, like me, is not fully satisfied with this youth's credentials. To allow him access to the treasury seems to me to be a foolhardy step but who am I to question Didda? Rakka seems very pleased and does not seem to have any ulterior motive in mind. And yet I wonder.

Naravahana is preoccupied with another issue, at the moment, as are the queen and the court. Some weeks ago, Yashodhara had embarked on a campaign against the Shahi ruler, Thakkana, the chief of a neighbouring hill region. Thakkana claims descent from the great Shahi family of Kabul and Gandhara to which Didda also belongs. Perhaps she was angered by his effrontery in claiming so and thus gave her consent to this campaign.

Yashodhara had also warned her that the army was restless and needed a battle to engage in or it might turn rebellious and unheeding of its master. Moreover, this was to be his first campaign after his appointment as commander-in-chief and it was clear that he wanted to prove himself, to demonstrate his prowess. We fear the worst now as there has been no information of the campaign all this while. After all, it is no easy task to vanquish Thakkana in an area notorious for its impassable streams and mountains, and for its ferocious warriors.

It is only on the day after Abhimanyu's wedding that the long-awaited news from Yashodhara reaches the court. Thakkana has been quelled and made to pay tribute; the campaign was an outright success. Didda is elated and announces a fresh round of celebrations, but by nightfall, her mood is sombre, bitter. And it is all the work of Rakka.

I am with her when he pours the requisite poison in her ears.

'Yashodhara has betrayed you,' he murmurs. 'I always suspected his motives and so, my spies had followed him to gather evidence. They have just returned in advance of the main army and they tell me that Yashodhara has taken money from Thakkana to keep him on the throne. Now he will return glorying in his victory and seeking vengeance for the way you treated his friends and fellow-plotters. Do you think, Queen Didda, that he has forgiven you? No, he hasn't and he never will.'

I see Didda's face turn stony, her eyes grim, and my heart sinks. She will extract retribution of the worst kind and there will be no mercy.

And so, when Yashodhara thunders back in triumph at the head of his troops, the royal guards attempt to arrest him near his residence. Aghast, he resists them and orders the army, now loyal to him, to support him against the queen. The banner of rebellion that was successfully folded away is unfurled once more.

Yashodhara marches on the palace and succeeds in barricading it, catching the guards by surprise, his troops surrounding us with silent menace.

It is at this moment of Didda's greatest crisis that news reaches us from Lohara. The travel-stained, weary messenger is allowed through into the palace because he bears urgent news. Now he kneels before Didda and she commands him to speak. When he finishes, her face is empty of all expression but her hand grips my shoulder as if she desperately seeks to draw from my own strength.

Her parents have been murdered by her cousin, Vigraharaja, whose thwarted ambitions clearly led to this murderous assault. Udayaraja, newly-married, managed to escape along with his wife, sound the alarm and round up the troops but Vigraha fled before they could capture him.

He was last seen making his way towards Kashmira.

THE EFFECTS OF POISON

DIDDA

I am a prisoner of my enemies. Through the heavy wooden doors of the barricaded palace, I can hear the shouts of battle on the street and I am told that the waters of the Vitasta are stained red with the blood of those slain. I am also told that a large section of the army has joined cause with Yashodhara, and that Hariraja and Subhadhara, known professional fighters, have decided to support him and swell his troops with their forces.

There is, nevertheless, a small but substantial section of the royal army that remains undecided, without mooring. Unsure whether to cast its lot with one or the other, it lounges by the palace gates, watching the fighting and perhaps waiting for orders that do not come. In a few days, I might be forced to make overtures to them, to win back a group of soldiers who should have been unflinchingly loyal to me, in any case. I have, on my side, the fierce Ekangas, the royal bodyguards, and the Tantrins, the royal foot soldiers, and together their might is formidable. I am grateful that they automatically support my cause—or rather, that of Abhimanyu.

Meanwhile, I find I have no time to mourn the passing away of my beloved mother. I do not spare a single thought for my father—we never loved each other and I feel no loss at his death—but she was my support even when we were no longer together. Her letters gave me confidence and cheer, and helped me believe that I would prevail over all my troubles. Now I feel as if I have been cast adrift on an enormous ocean that threatens to fight me, sink me, overwhelm me, annihilate me.

Another worry that tears away at me is of Udayaraja's safety. I know that my grandfather will do all he can to muster support for him but I cannot stop fretting. I am also filled with anger at my dastardly cousin, Vigraharaja, who scarcely merits a family tie after his unforgivable deed. I hope that the reports of him heading for Kashmira are false. Yet, at the same time, I find myself wishing that he falls into my clutches someday so that I can crush him with the might of my newfound power, although it is fast slipping through my fingers.

I fear that I might have lost everything through haste. Rakka keeps out of my way; he knows he is in disgrace for giving me wrong counsel and filling my ears with unfounded accusations. Yet in my heart, I know I am equally to blame. What made me believe in Rakka without a moment's reflection? Why should I have automatically assumed that Yashodhara was a traitor? I know now that I have misjudged his strength, his popularity and his pride. All he was looking for was a chance to prove his loyalty and now I have pushed him into becoming a rebel. How stupid I was not to understand this!

Naravahana's reproachful silences are even harder to bear. However, his palpable fury against Rakka is justified. I thought that Rakka was a blundering old fool, not a malicious one. I had only used him to prove a point to Phalguna and his supporters. I wanted to show them that they were redundant in the new scheme of things, that I had several supporters at my beck and call to step into their shoes and govern Kashmira. Yet in doing so, have I made a mistake? Am I standing close to ruin? Have I lost Abhimanyu his throne?

Abhimanyu is in hiding again, this time with his wife to accompany him; Naravahana rushed them to the Bhattarakamatha even as Yashodhara's forces were hemming us in. I owe my son's life to him—he knows this—yet he does not look for words of gratitude or praise. He simply executes his duty and I know I am truly blessed in his loyalty. Yet I can't suppress a prickle of irritation when I reflect upon his words. How is it that he is always right? How is it that he judges people with such exactitude? And how is it that I lack this ability?

As I reflect thus, Naravahana comes to me as if I have summoned him by my thoughts. He bows and I gesture to him to speak, my eyes turning to the window and the sounds of fighting outside.

'I have managed to recruit some mercenaries with the promise of riches,' he says, 'but your treasury will be depleted if this goes on.'

I turn my gaze towards him, smoothing my silk robes with my sweating hands. Valga, silent and observant, is by my side as usual and I see her tense as if she anticipates an argument between us. 'I know that this cannot go on for ever,' I tell him curtly. 'What do you advise?'

'We need more soldiers,' he says quietly. 'Superior numbers will sway the result. Then we can force Yashodhara to surrender. But it is proving to be a difficult task to get them.'

'What do we do?' I ask him. 'Can we bargain with Yashodhara? Can we find a weak spot to pounce upon?'

'You have treated him unfairly,' he points out with brutal frankness. 'He now commands troops who are disaffected and ripe for rebellion. We don't really have a way out.'

I wonder if he is saying this to punish me for my recklessness. I square my shoulders and stiffen my back. Valga moves to my side but I wave her away.

'There is always a way out,' I respond, softly but firmly. 'And I will find it.'

He looks so weary that I suspect he has not slept for days on end—but his face lifts with hope at my words.

I am filled with regret that I have brought matters to this pass but all the more determined to break the impasse and return to normalcy. I sit alone in my darkened chamber and cudgel my brains that have hitherto led me out of impossible circumstances. At first, I despair when no solution suggests itself to me. However, at long last, I discern the glimmerings of hope. There *is* a simple but effective way to break the back of the rebels who have captured the city—and I think I have found it.

I summon Naravahana around midnight, and instruct him to round up the food merchants of Shrinagara and bring them before me somehow. I do not worry about how he will do this; he has never let me down before and I trust him to find a way.

He does—and in just under an hour, he brings them before me. They are six in number and together they provide the people's daily food needs. All of them have been clandestinely involved in supplying Yashodhara's troops with rice and wheat, with fruit and vegetables, with meat and fish—and guilt is writ large on their faces. A few minutes is all it takes—a few minutes to tell them the dire consequences of feeding the rebels and the route they must now take to redeem themselves in my eyes. Death is the only alternative I give them.

And so, the deed is done, the die is cast. As one day follows another, Yashodhara's army begins to starve. Their suppliers have mysteriously vanished, their shops are barricaded or shut down altogether and there is absolutely no food to be had even with the lure of money. The more we intimidate the merchants, the faster they comply with our orders and, in no time at all, we have demolished Yashodhara's challenge and destroyed his famished army's spirit.

They withdraw, fearing an onslaught which they scarcely have the strength to face but I do not spare them. My troops follow at their heels, and force them to turn and give battle. A man needs a full stomach to fight but theirs have been empty for days. They fight valiantly, braving their dizziness, their weakness, but it is over very quickly. A roar goes up from my men when Hariraja falls from his horse and is captured. Yashodhara struggles on but his sword breaks as he fights and he is forced to submit along with the rest of his force.

This time, I adopt measures which will dissuade any future rebel from challenging me. My plan is one of calculated revenge. Yashodhara and the other ringleaders have their heads chopped off in full public view and their bodies thrown into the Vitasta with large stones bound to their necks. I force their family members and relatives to watch so that they know exactly where the foolhardiness of their men has led them. Some of them fall at my feet, crying for mercy. I grant it, offering Subhadhara's wife and daughter positions in the palace. I ignore the others, particularly Yashodhara's pale-eyed wife who does not shed a single tear but looks at me as if she would like to impale me with her gaze. I admire her fortitude but dismiss her from my mind. She is powerless now that her husband is dead. What ill can she do to me on her own?

I return the command of the army to Rakka but also demote him from the rank of prime minister. He does not protest at this or at my elevation of Naravahana to the title of Rajanaka. Now the latter is next only to Abhimanyu and me in status, and the most powerful official post in Kashmira is in his capable hands.

'I do not deserve this, Queen Didda,' he tells me softly as I am walking out of the throne room. His face is flushed with gratitude, his eyes gleam with loyalty.

'You have served me well, my dear friend,' I respond. 'And this is your reward.'

He bows and steps aside.

117

That night, he throws a feast in my honour. The cooks scurry to and fro bearing enormous platters of fragrant rice flavoured with walnuts and apples, of curries floating in succulent gravies, of sweetmeats made with the choicest almonds. I do not have much of an appetite after my recent travails but I sample each dish because each mouthful I take seems to fill him with happiness and satisfaction.

This meal seems to herald a trend in the court before very long. All the important officers and courtiers vie with each other to hold feasts in my honour and thereby proclaim their loyalty to me. I indulge them for I do not want to shame anyone by refusing. Nevertheless, I ensure that I do not favour one over the other.

Rakka, meanwhile, continues to keep a low profile and is surprisingly subdued when Naravahana inspects the troops regularly on my orders and reports to me on the army expenditure. He is in charge of every other department of administration as well, so he is busier than he has ever been before. Yet he never complains of fatigue or lassitude. His eyes shine with happiness when I praise him; his voice rings out with increasing confidence when he reports to me. He is more solicitous than ever about my health and well-being, and sometimes his concern borders on the annoying.

'Naravahana fusses over me like an old man,' I laugh to Valga as she combs my long hair. 'He is getting to be a bore, isn't he?'

I am facing the mirror and so, am completely mystified by the sudden anger I see flashing across her usually passive face.

'It is fortunate that so many people care about you, Queen Didda,' she says tightly. 'Him as well.'

I frown and look down at my fingers, puzzling over her words. What has made her so furious? Could she be *jealous*? No, that is a laughable thought! She has never shown any signs of it in all these days, after all.

I raise my eyes to her reflection in the mirror. 'Have you ever thought of getting married, Valga?' I ask.

'I am too old,' she says promptly.

'No, you aren't. If you wanted, I could look around for a suitable man.'

She shrugs and smiles. 'Who would look after you then? Who would carry you around?'

There is no trace of anger on her face now. I wonder again what had prompted it earlier.

Sindhu, the treasurer, comes to me two days later. It is for a mundane reason—an assent for a trifling item of expenditure.

'Why do you trouble me over such a small matter?' I ask irritably.

'Should I have asked the Rajanaka Naravahana instead, your majesty?' His face is bland but something about his tone infuriates me.

'What do you mean?' I bristle.

'It is so confusing, Queen Didda,' he says smoothly, his voice almost oily in its evenness. 'The king does not give orders because you are ruling in his name. But now it seems as if the Rajanaka is all-in-all. At least, that is what everyone says.'

His words linger in my mind long after the conversation, long after I have dismissed Sindhu and sent him on his way, long after they should have remained. Thus it is that when Naravahana comes before me that evening, my mood is black, my mind throbbing with unwanted thoughts. I am peremptory with him, even rude, and I see his eyes darken with hurt.

I cannot sleep that night, worry eating into my repose, uncertainty filling my thoughts. Have I given Naravahana too much power? Will he turn against me some day like the other rebels? Will the lure of greater power change his loyalties?

I remain undecided the following morn but the doubts persist all day and on the days that follow. I am curt with Naravahana, abrasive and dismissive, and I know he cannot fathom the reason for my altered behaviour. Valga is baffled, too; any day now she will ask me what the matter is. And I am not sure how to answer her. How do I describe the terror that has me in its grip?

When Naravahana finally plucks up the courage to ask me what is wrong, I brush him aside, leaving him as unclear as before. How do I cast my doubts into words? How can I tell Naravahana that it is fear that consumes me—fear that I will lose his loyalty some day; fear that I will lose my oldest friend to greed, to power wrangles; fear that he will change sides, leaving me alone as I was before he came along?

He invites me to his chambers for the evening meal, perhaps hoping to recreate our earlier affection. I am still debating whether to accept or decline, whether to meet him and confess my doubts and ascertain his loyalty—or to leave matters as they are. I dismiss Valga and begin dressing slowly, twisting my long hair that has begun to grey into a coil, holding my jewellery against my skin to determine what looks best on me.

When Sindhu begs entry, at this point, I am still rehearsing the words that I propose to say to Naravahana and so I can't quite understand what he is trying to tell me at first.

'Repeat yourself,' I command.

His face is red and he is breathless as if he has been running fast. 'My master, Rakka, is worried about you,

Queen Didda,' he pants. 'He fears that Naravahana has plotted to kill you. He thinks he will do it when you are feasting in his chambers tonight, after which he will arrest your attendants. My master has been suspecting him for some time. He begs you to believe him.'

The demons rise again in my mind, crowding it with terror. I dismiss Sindhu without a word and send word to Naravahana that I will not attend his feast. Then I lie down upon my couch, torn between doubt and suspicion, and straining my ears, every now and then, for the fearful clanking of soldiers' swords along the passage.

As the hours pass, I find myself becoming more composed, more at ease. My fears lose their frightening grip on my mind and my heart ceases to pound. I should have had more sense than to believe Rakka again!

Tomorrow Naravahana and I will talk, I tell myself. I will talk to him about these stupid rumours and laugh with him at my fears. I will beg his forgiveness for doubting him. And all will be well between us again.

Naravahana is found hanging in his chambers at dawn. His face is purple with clotted blood; his neck is swollen where the rope has bitten into it all night. He has left a letter, addressed to me.

I see no point in living, it says, *when I have faulted you in some way. I have thought through my actions and cannot understand the*

reason for your anger. Yet I beg your forgiveness for any lapse of mine
and pray that you will always remember my loyalty to you.

VALGA

She has killed him. She has taken his life as surely as if she had wound the cord around his neck and tightened the knot so that his life ebbed away. I feel bereft, alone, weighed down by sorrow so crushing that I cannot lift my head under its weight. He will never smile at me again, he will never again ask me how I am, he will never again walk by my side as we follow her footsteps.

I take to my bed, listening to the cries of horror in the courtyard below me as the news reaches more and more people in the palace. I hear the summons for the priests, I hear the women come to wash and anoint his lifeless body, I hear the thud of logs being piled one atop another to make his pyre.

The maids come to my room, anxious, solicitous, for I am never ill. I turn my face away from them, the tears just behind my aching eyes. The light of the sun stabs me with fresh grief. He will never see the sun again, this beloved friend of mine.

She does not send for me and I do not care what she has been told. All day I lie unmoving on my bed, my mind grappling with what has happened, allowing grief to seep into me in tiny fragments so that it does not overwhelm me all at once. My tears still remain unshed, a dull weight behind my eyes.

Towards evening, I hear the prayers being chanted around his pyre, I hear the flames crackling as they consume his body, I hear the silence that descends as the mourners disperse and his ashes are left to cool. His father had died many years ago and I wonder who has performed his last rites. Perhaps a courtier who has been made to stand in for his family?

My maids come again, twittering around me like witless birds, wondering why it is that I won't eat, coaxing me to sit up, offering to fetch the physician. I send them away, telling them not to fret, that I will be better tomorrow. The lie slides out of my mouth easily, effortlessly. In any case, it is convincing enough for they leave forthwith, and I am left in darkness and solitude once more.

She comes in the early hours of dawn. A part of me has been expecting her, so I am not surprised. The palace is sunk in slumber and the sound of her breathing is loud in the resultant quiet. I rise to my feet, ignoring the lightheadedness of my weakened body.

'Are you ill?' she asks, her voice lower than usual.

'Yes.'

'What ails you?'

'You know what ails me.' In all these years, I have never spoken to her in this tone but I am suffused with rage and this has made me reckless.

She lays a hand on my shoulder. 'It was not my fault, Valga.'

I flinch at her touch and she snatches her hand away as if I have stung her.

'He trusted you,' I hiss in a furious whisper. 'No one could have been as devoted. And what was his reward? Your doubts, your anger, your accusations, your ...'

'I would have spoken to him,' she says, a catch in her voice. 'How did I know he would go so far?'

'It's too late, Queen Didda,' I say savagely. 'Too late to bring him back.'

She looks at me, her eyes pleading, but I do not relent. Later, when I am calmer, I realise that she could have had me arrested or exiled for my behaviour but she does none of those things. Instead, she turns to go and at the doorway, she says quietly, 'I loved him, too. He was a dear friend. My oldest one.' And then she is enveloped by the darkness.

On the morrow, everything is different. I resume my duties at her side and we make no allusion to the conversation of the night. It is as if it had never taken place. Serving her has become my life, I know no other way of living. And so, I go on as before.

The first thing she does is to summon Rakka and his henchman, Sindhu, and they stand before her, blanching in fear, guilt swamping their features.

'You tried to mislead me,' she says and there is something in her tone that makes them tremble with dread. She gestures to her guards. 'Cut off their heads and throw their bodies outside the city walls for the dogs to feed on. This is the fate they deserve.'

Sindhu screams and falls to his feet in a vain bid for forgiveness but the guards haul him upright and drag him away. His cries and pleas can be heard long after he leaves; they mingle with the shouts of the guards and the horrified shrieks of some serving girls who are witness to this scene. Rakka, on the other hand, offers no resistance; perhaps he realises that he has pushed his luck too far. He allows himself to be led away, his shoulders hunched in resignation.

Didda's act has the effect of quenching all the whispers and gossip in court. None want to displease her; none want to risk incurring her wrath. All day, she carries on with her duties as normal but is quieter than usual. When dusk falls, she dismisses all her other attendants and turns to me.

'Take his ashes,' she says, 'and do as you see fit with them. I have lost the right to claim him as my own.'

I take the carved jar from her hands and bow my head.

Later, I walk down to the banks of the Vitasta. Night has fallen and the waters are black, gleaming now and then where they catch the lights of the palace. The tide is coming in and if I do not hasten, I might be swept away by the strong current and drown in its unseen depths. I bend low over the river and tip the contents of the jar into her. The greyness mingles with the waters till the ashes are swept away.

I shake the jar again to empty it. The wind snatches at my hand and blows some ashes onto my face. I rub the soft layer that has covered my cheeks like a caress. Then I wash my hands in the waters and step back, the sadness lifting a little from my heart. I look up at the sky as the waves tug playfully at my feet. There are no stars, only a thick cover of clouds, and the air is heavy with an impending storm.

'Look after him,' I entreat the gods. 'Let his soul rest in peace.'

The tears come then, shocking me with their violence, rocking me with their intensity. I scramble away from the waters and collapse onto the rocky ground, shaking with sobs. I do not know how long I lie there but I cry until every last tear has been wrenched out of me and then I make my way back to the palace. The weight behind my eyes has lifted; his loss seems more bearable now.

When I have wiped away the stains of my tears and washed my face with cold, bracing water, I make my way to her chambers. She is surrounded by her attendants who are preparing her for sleep, a chore that is usually mine. As soon as she sees me, however, she waves them away and we are left alone.

'I immersed them in the Vitasta,' I tell her. 'This was his home, he loved Kashmira, so I thought it the best way.'

She nods, looking at her fingers that are entwined on her lap.

'If I said something harsh the other day,' I add, 'it was because I was upset. Please forgive me for those words.'

She nods again and then looks up and I am struck dumb by her eyes. They are cold and lifeless, empty of all emotion. As I stare into them, they change; now they are dark, with unreadable depths. I give an involuntary cry and step forward.

'Do you feel all right?' I ask worriedly. 'You don't look ...'

'Nothing is the same,' she cuts me short. 'And it never will be.'

I linger, unsure what to say, unclear about the meaning of her words.

'Nothing means anything to me anymore,' she goes on after a pause, 'but this land, this throne, my destiny. Remember that, Valga, for I will not say it again.'

I stare at her, wondering what she means, once more. I do not know whether to agree with her or remain silent or even to turn away. She looks up again and my eyes fasten on hers. Something flares in them and I take a step back without quite realising what I'm doing.

And my heart quails inwardly at the ferocity and ruthlessness that I have read in them.

THE THRONE OF DEATH

DIDDA

Time passes, sometimes in a rush but more often slowly and inexorably. I have now mastered the art of blocking out portions of my mind at will, especially when I do not want to dwell on disturbing memories—and there are many of them. I focus all my energies on the land and its governance, and have taken to conducting surprise inspections of officers and the departments under their jurisdiction. Consequently, the sight of me causes many to tremble and I rejoice in this power. There is no more shirking, no more tardiness, no more incompetence.

And, most importantly, there are no more challenges to my rule.

Abhimanyu remains a figurehead. He knows that he has disappointed me in his aversion to the throne, in his reluctance to run the kingdom, in his incomprehension of politics and strategy. He is now the sole parent to three boys, for his frail wife died after their third child was born. He spends his time cooped up in his chambers with his children, supervising their education and gently harrying the royal tutors with his scholarly suggestions.

My son has cast his three sons in his mould. They are pale-faced, timid, studious, inclined to avoid all manner of rough talk and action. I see a spark sometimes in Bhimagupta, the youngest, but Nandigupta and Tribhuvana, who will precede him to the throne, are insipid, meek characters. They fear me for I do not hide my impatience and I know that my weekly visits to them are ordeals to be endured.

This crop of children is a poor inheritance for Kashmira. They will wreck all that has been achieved by their ancestors, by me. I cannot allow this to happen for the sake of the realm. I have to do something. I have to find a solution.

Soon after Rakka's death, I summoned Phalguna to court and he stood before me, expectant yet wary.

'I need your help again,' I began without preamble.

'May I ask what has happened in my absence for you to recall me from Parnotsa, your majesty?' he asked softly.

'May I ask if your network of spies has ever failed you in their information?' I retorted and was gratified to see him flush with embarrassment.

His demeanour changed abruptly—now he stood straight-backed with all his courtly dignity flooding back into his body.

'I need you to be my prime minister again,' I said.

He nodded and bowed. 'It would be an honour,' he murmured.

Nothing more was said: nothing about his grandsons that I had executed, his daughters that I had exiled, his family that I had brought to its knees. Nothing about his time spent away from court in exile with his son, about the hours he must have spent chafing at his ruin. Neither he nor I have ever wasted time on words. Ours is a professional pact, a dealing that is mutually beneficial— and both of us know that.

He took up his duties the very same day and slid smoothly back into his duties. I was relieved of the pressure of inspections, of the countless checks around the kingdom. He took it over from me and I knew without question that the post was in safe hands. Moreover, I had no need to fear any betrayals or reprisals from him. He was virtually alone, hitherto isolated by my hand, and now he drew his sustenance and power from me alone.

It is Phalguna who brings me news of Abhimanyu's ailment. My son has been complaining of malaise but there is no immediate cause to pinpoint. As days go by, he has prolonged bouts of coughing and sickness, and grows weaker and weaker. The physicians try everything—from simple food to strong physic—but after a fortnight, it is clear that the situation is serious.

I visit him often, ignoring his boys who sit wide-eyed and quiet as mice in a corner of his chamber. My eyes are all for my son, my beautiful boy whose once-smooth brow is now creased with pain, whose beautiful eyes are dark with misery. On the day he fails to recognise me, I know the end is near.

I leave his rooms and the cloying smell of herbs within that fail to combat the stench of illness. My hands are trembling and I am panting as if I have been running.

Once in my chambers, I dismiss my attendants, even Valga, though she throws me a questioning glance, and sit alone in the silence. I think of what I have done and the course ahead of me, the path that I must now adopt. I think of Kashmira, this beautiful land that has become mine, and of the ways I have tried to strengthen it. I think of the people of this land who have grown to respect me and now greet me with genuine love.

And then I think about my destiny, of the astrologer's prediction of my greatness, of my instinct that I am nearing it. I think hard, my hands clenched in concentration, my mind pushing out every other thought and calmness slowly steals over me. My hands grow steady, my breathing returns to normal and my mind isn't ravaged by doubt any more.

When they come to tell me of Abhimanyu's death, they are taken aback by my serenity.

I rise to see my son one last time. He was not meant for this world. He was not meant to deal with its wickedness; with the company of those who would wither him, like the sun does the Shirisha flower. Now he belongs to the gods, as he should.

Nandigupta, ten and desolate, steps onto the throne. He is fearful of his own shadow and is dwarfed by the royal seat, his legs dangling above the floor, his thin body perched on the very edge. I have no time to still his apprehensions, to chivvy him into regality, for I am in the throes of a new obsession that descends on me without warning.

I have identified a portion of land on the outskirts of Shrinagara where I will buid a memorial to my son. I spend a part of each day supervising the clearing of the land and the building of a temple to Lord Vishnu within the complex. It takes many months but I am persistent and patient. Thus does the town of Abhimanyupura come into existence, adorned by its beautiful temple of Abhimanyusvamin.

As I walk around the shining edifice, it strikes me that concretising one's power on the physical landscape is a worthy course to pursue. While I am alive and even after I am gone, it will remind people constantly of my presence, my achievements.

Phalguna, who has additional charge of the royal finances, makes no protest when I dig deep into the treasury to fund more towns, more shrines, for he knows that our coffers will be speedily replenished, in any case. Kashmira is prosperous and this is immediately discernible to the eye. Its lush crop-laden fields, its magnificent cities and thriving villages, its well-fed and well-clothed citizens, bear ample testimony to this fact.

I build the town of Diddapura after my name with its temple of Diddasvamin dedicated to Lord Vishnu. To house the immigrants flooding to Kashmira from other places—from Madhyadesha, Lata and Saudotra— seeking work and wealth, I build a colossal matha in the centre of Shrinagara and this, in turn, attracts many more migrants. I throw myself into these efforts with a frenzy; it is like I am possessed. Stones, wood, building material and designs are the things that occupy my mind now—and this, fortunately, builds a strong wall around my grief.

My building efforts have paid off. Through the length and breadth of this land, people hail me for my piety, for my nobility of thought and deed, for my purity of soul. I am achieving new heights of popularity, rapidly becoming invincible, invulnerable.

An entire year goes by in this exercise and by the end of it, I have marked my presence in every part of Kashmira.

I call Valga to me and put a purse of money into her hands. She is startled and slightly wary.

'I want you to construct something, too,' I tell her. 'Build a temple, a shrine, a town, anything you like.'

'Why?'

The question is a simple one but leaves me struggling for words.

'I have no desire for fame,' she adds quietly.

I take her hands in mine, troubled by the sadness that perpetually marks her face these days. 'Do it for me,' I urge. 'It will make me happy. I want my Valga to be known to everyone, a name to be uttered with reverence.'

She obeys me, in due course, and the Valgamatha is unobtrusive like her, built on an edge of ill-frequented land in the northeastern corner of Shrinagara. She throws it open to the poor migrants of the city and uses all her money to feed and clothe them, and to educate their children. It is almost as if she is seeking atonement for some misdeed. When I question her, though, she denies it but her eyes tell me that I am right. I do not pursue the matter further; Valga is entitled to her secrets, after all.

I finally turn my attention to Nandigupta, my grandson and figure-king, who mounts the throne each day with increasing trepidation. His face has assumed an unhealthy pallor, his silken clothes seem to hang on his skinny frame. He picks at his food, rejecting almost everything that is placed before him.

'Do you fear poison?' I ask him coldly when he refuses to touch the day's choice preparation, causing the cook to look visibly disappointed.

He turns big, frightened eyes on me and his face is alive with dread. It is one of those rare occasions when we are dining together—and it seems to be as much of an ordeal for him now as before he became king. I stifle the fierce irritation that courses through me. 'Your food is tasted *before* it is brought to you,' I say slowly. 'You have no need to worry.'

'My appetite is fading,' he falters and then goes on. 'I have no desire for food these days.'

I click my tongue. 'This can't go on,' I say. 'I will send you something to soothe your stomach.'

And I do. For the next fortnight, I send him concoctions of herbs through his attendant every night. They are prepared by my physician on my specific orders and no one is allowed to view the ingredients during the process. I instruct Nandigupta's attendant to keep me apprised of his master's progress and his reports are positive. The medicine is clearly effective; Nandigupta seems more energetic, more robust, and seems to have turned a corner.

Until the day he collapses while on his way to the throne-room and the physician is unable to find a pulse. I am summoned by his fevered attendant, whose mouth is slack with horror, his lips hardly able to frame the necessary words.

'The king . . . the king is dying,' he falters.

Beside me, Valga exhales in shock and grips my arm involuntarily. I draw a deep breath and we hasten in the attendant's wake to where Nandigupta's small body lies just below the throne, his face serene and still.

'It was his heart,' the physician informs me, looking shaken. 'It stopped beating before we could do anything. I am afraid the king, your grandson, is dead.'

I look around me. The courtiers are stiff with dismay, horror slowly flooding their faces. It is perhaps the suddenness of his death that has unnerved them—or the fact of his death itself. Two royal deaths in quick succession would unnerve any court.

The physician looks disturbed, unsure about something. He catches my eye and opens his mouth to speak.

'Prepare the body for the funeral,' I instruct the attendants. I do not wish to hear anything that he has to say. My heart beats faster. Too many thoughts are whirling around in my mind for me to dwell overlong on what has happened, to grasp the sheer enormity of this occurrence. I issue more crisp orders mechanically and then turn to walk out of the room.

It is then that my eye catches that of Tribhuvana, my second grandson and Nandigupta's younger brother, who is partly in the shadows, holding on tightly to Bhimagupta, the youngest. There is a look of terror on his face and his hand involuntarily rises as if to shield himself. From me. For he is the next in line to the throne.

VALGA

My dreams slash through my sleep and hurtle me to a startled wakefulness, my skin drenched in sweat despite the cold of the night, my heart pounding like a caged creature in my body. Each one is worse than the last and the torment is beginning to show on my face.

'Are you ill?' she asks me.

How can I tell her that she is responsible for my nightmares? How can I tell her that my head is bursting with suspicions, with half-formed doubts, with fear of what lies ahead? How can I tell her that when I see her face, it is the face of my dreams, the face that belongs to a black heart?

Yet when I see her face creased with concern for me, feel the gentle touch of her hands on my face, look into her worry-filled eyes, I want to shake and slap myself. How can this woman be a murderer? How can someone so affectionate kill her own kin? No, I tell myself sternly, I can't blame her for those deaths. They were unfortunate but destined to happen—and I must stop my mind from rioting just because I am upset.

Instead, I plunge into my works of charity with so much zeal that I feel faint at the end of each day. Yet this is the only thing that lifts my heart, the only aspect of my life that I can be proud of, the only thing that reassures me in my goodness.

I look closely at Tribhuvana, the newly-anointed king and unwilling successor of his beloved older brother. He is so like Nandigupta in looks and demeanour that it is as if nothing has changed and that the latter is still alive. His eyes follow his grandmother wherever she goes and they are filled with resignation, with hopelessness—unlike the fear that leaped in Nandigupta's own. I want to hug this boy, to hold him tightly in my arms and reassure him that he will be safe, that I will watch over him, that it is wrong for him to look so bleak at such a tender age.

I watch her closely, too. There is nothing that I can fault in her manner except for her usual abruptness and impatience. But this is the way she always is. In fact, her mood is rather mellow, at the moment, owing to good tidings from her home. News does not come from Lohara with its earlier frequency and so, it is all the more precious for being so rare. Udayaraja now has a third son and it seems likely that his healthy wife will produce many more, an entire brood. She is a girl from Gandhara who was chosen by King Bhima Shahi as his grandson's bride. They have never visited us as a couple but, by all accounts, she is cheerful and bright, and clearly adored by her husband. This is enough to make Didda content and relieved.

I think of Naravahana often but it still hurts to relive memories. Perhaps some day when I am much older, I will be able to remember him without pain, without regret, with peace. Meanwhile, there is much to occupy me—my chores at court beside Didda and later, the supervision of my matha. My physical strength remains unabated and I am grateful for that, yet I cannot say the same for my mental endurance. It seems as if I live each day poised on a tightrope between regret and fear; the one for the past, the other of the future.

On the day that Tribhuvana falls from his horse and dies, I am away from Shrinagara. Didda had given me permission to visit the shrines of Vijayeshvara, a day's ride from the capital city, and I had set out eagerly with a single attendant. The journey was pleasant, my sacred mission fruitful, and I embark on the return journey, feeling serene after a long time and exulting in this uncommon feeling.

As I near Shrinagara, I realise, with a pang, that something is wrong. People are huddled by the roads looking distraught and conversing in agitated voices. The lamps to mark the path have not been lit and the way ahead is a dark abyss. My heart starts to pound and my hands, slick with sweat, slip more than once from the reins. I gallop ahead, muddled prayers echoing in my head, futilely hoping that all is well.

Gripped with a terrible anxiety, I ride into the palace courtyard and jump from the horse, staggering as I almost fall.

'Take care. This is how he died!' observes a stablehand drily, emerging from the shadows and taking hold of the reins.

'Who?' I cry. 'Who?'

'King Tribhuvana. He fell from his horse today while out on a hunt. He hit his head on a rock and died on the spot.'

In the days that follow, I try to shut my ears to the whispers and rumours that float in the air like dry leaves in a summer wind. Who gave Tribhuvana permission to hunt when he was clearly too young for it? Was it true that his saddle had not been fastened properly, that the reins were deliberately loose? Wasn't it odd that his attendants hadn't accompanied him on the hunt, that he only had two newly-recruited courtiers with him?

My fears and doubts are back, all over again, to haunt me through my waking hours and then kill my sleep through frightening dreams. I have failed this little boy. I had wanted to protect him, to reassure him, but his fate had already been written and sealed. It is my fault. Or is it?

I long to approach her with my misgivings and accusations, however unfounded they might be, but I restrain myself. Her mood is foul, malicious, unpredictable—and there are two deaths responsible for this. The first is that of her beloved grandfather, King Bhima Shahi, in Gandhara. I know that she mourns his loss more than that of Tribhuvana. The second—Phalguna—affects both her and the kingdom. He died a few days after the news from Gandhara reached us, depriving Kashmira of a strong, steady governing hand.

Bhimagupta, Abhimanyu's youngest child, is on the throne now. He is eleven, older than his brothers were when they became king, and definitely not as naïve as them. He is wary and stubborn, clearly the only one of the three who can stand up to her if the need arises. When he looks at her, his eyes are dark with blame, remembering his brothers' sudden deaths. She finds him sullen and unbiddable, cynical beyond his years. Nevertheless, the same pattern persists—she rules, he is the figurehead. He knows there are limits to his defiance. I ache with sympathy for him—so alone and isolated, and so impossibly brave.

It is in the early days of Bhimagupta's rule that Tunga enters the court. Tall and fair with green eyes, he immediately draws all attention to him and an amused smile curves his lips, as if he knows the effect of his appearance on others. He is a lekhaharaka, a letter carrier, who has come to Shrinagara from Parnotsa. He belongs to the Khasha tribe, as does the ruling family of Lohara, and I see Didda's interest quicken when he states his ancestry.

Tunga is one among five brothers but the only one bold enough to journey to the court at Shrinagara and request a job. He will do anything, he says.

'I have even herded buffaloes when I was a youth,' he declares.

'Then why come to the court and not a farm?' retorts Didda. Nevertheless, she is clearly impressed by his confidence, by his straightforwardness.

144

He smiles at her and bows low. 'Because I am also a scribe, Queen Didda. I taught myself to read and write, and that is why I was entrusted with the delivery of important missives. I can even write poetry of a very high order.'

'What this court needs,' Didda says, 'is not a poet but an administrator. Are you one?'

Tunga smiles. 'I possess just the skills you are looking for. After my days as a letter carrier, I turned my hand to governance. I was in charge of my native village of Baddivasa and two others besides. I collected revenue for the officers, made rules, ensured that . . .'

'That is all I need to know for the moment,' she breaks in. 'I will give you a post at this court that befits you.'

And so it begins. At first, he is given trifling jobs and then, as the days wear on, more responsible ones that involve the overseeing of expenditure, the inspection of the city, the submission of reports on infrastructure. It is soon apparent to everyone that he enjoys her special favour. By degrees, he is even allowed an audience with her whenever he desires it.

Tunga begins to flaunt these special privileges like his personal flag. He is smug and arrogant, openly critical of those who would challenge him. There are subdued murmurs of discontent at court but none dare to openly voice their disapproval. They hope that he will eventually go Rakka's way—rising to dizzy heights and ending his days on a garbage heap.

'Valga, do you disapprove of me?' he asks me boldly as he passes me in the palace one morning.

I stop and stare at him, not troubling to conceal my dislike.

He steps closer. 'I know what you're thinking but you misjudge me,' he says softly. 'I am not out for money or position. I merely seek to serve my queen.'

'You serve the king,' I snap.

'You know who the real ruler is,' he says impatiently. 'Why do you think I came to this court? She has made this kingdom what it is—strong, prosperous, a place where a man can be known for his worth.'

Later, I wonder whether this is true. Is this her reputation outside our borders? And is it stronger than all the rumours? Is this how people actually perceive her?

And in my heart, I know that his words make sense. Kashmira in the days of Kshemagupta was weak, riven by warring factions, known for its bad governance, a tempting prize for a stronger power. Kashmira in the time of Didda is powerful, invulnerable, a much-sought-after ally, a place of impeccable governance. She has made it so—and this is perhaps her destiny.

As months and then years roll by, and Bhimagupta remains secure on the throne, I allow myself to hope that he will live long, that he will be spared in some way. He is fifteen now, nearly old enough to rule on his own, mature enough to take the right decisions and govern his kingdom well. Perhaps he has relaxed his vigil, too, for he looks so much more stable, more secure. He is still surly around his grandmother but perhaps this is prompted by vestiges of his earlier fears and he will come to respect her in time.

I persist in my hopes even when I hear of his arrest a few days before he turns sixteen. I am in my matha and absorbed in some work when I am told of what has transpired at court in my absence. Bhimagupta challenged his grandmother about Tunga, it seems. He accused her of favouring Tunga unduly, of allowing him to exploit her and the treasury and his people, of not having the sense to discriminate between right and wrong. My heart sinks as I hear this. She will never forgive him for his words—I know her well enough to know this with a damning certainty.

Bhimagupta dies in prison on the day that Tunga is made the prime minister at court. No one bothers to investigate his death; no one dares to ask how it happened. It seems as if I am the only one who cares, the only one whose heart is breaking with sorrow and remorse, the only one who feels so tarnished by sin that its weight makes my body sag.

Yet I know this much—that I am not the only one who knows the reason for his death.

THE NOOSE OF KINSHIP

DIDDA

It is cold and the sky is heavy with the weight of unshed snow. The world is bathed in hues of black and white. The ground is hard as iron and rings a tune when I step on it. I huddle closer in my woollen cloak and pull down the sleeves so that they cover my hands. Now it is as if I am crippled in another way. I laugh and pull the sleeves back, flexing my fingers and then looking closely at the lines that crisscross my palm. What do they mean? Is it true that they tell the future, as I have heard some people say? How can a single crease in my skin claim that I will be rich or poor or fortunate? I shake my head and stare out at the gardens.

I hear footsteps behind me but I know who it is.

'What are you looking at so closely?' he asks.

'Nothing,' I say without turning around.

Flakes have begun to fall from the sky and I can feel them flutter against my face. They cover the ground, layer upon layer, in a soft, white cloak. I feel, once more, the onrush of joy that grips me every winter when its harsh yet beautiful touch finds an echo in my heart.

'I heard you laugh. You are happy.' It is a statement, not a question. I nod and turn to him, spreading my arms wide to encompass everything around me, the entire landscape.

'All this is mine,' I say with quiet satisfaction. 'This is my land. I am its ruler.'

'And you have been for a while,' he points out.

I shake my head. There is a difference between ruling in the name of another—deferring to him, waiting in the shadows—and becoming a ruler in one's own right.

I have finally achieved the latter. I am now king and queen in one. Kashmira belongs to me and mine.

Tunga's face darkens with worry. 'The people ...' he begins hesitantly.

'Will accept me.' My voice rings with conviction. There is no room for doubt here.

'They say ...'

'I know what they say,' I retort, almost savagely, 'but they know this land is safe in my hands—and I will command their respect for this.'

I am not insensible to the rumours that fly thick and fast around me, to the knowing glances on people's faces when they think I'm not looking, to the fear that leaps into their eyes when they are before me. This is particularly true of the male officials in my court. They do not know what to make of a female king, a woman who transgresses the norms to wield power, a woman who does not hide her gender in male garb but flaunts her beauty and femininity like a weapon. And yet, I find they are easy to manipulate once their fears have been lulled, once they are complacent. Then they are always eager to do my bidding.

Tunga continues to look troubled and I study his face covertly while he looks into the distance. He has transformed himself since coming to court. Once brash and cocksure, he is now a dignified, attentive courtier. He does not shirk responsibility, and shows both mental acuity in judgment and physical prowess in battle. He is proving to be my most dependable minister; almost like Naravahana, I think, feeling the inevitable pang of loss that shakes me whenever I allow myself to recall him.

'Don't trust this man,' he would tell me. 'How do you know what his motives are?'

'But I *do* trust him,' I speak to Naravahana in my mind. 'There is something in him that reminds me of you.'

Tunga gestures towards the palace, and I nod and smile. As we walk back together, the snow starts falling with a vengeance. The roads will be impassable tonight, I think, and I will have to post extra soldiers at the border gates to guard against attacks that might use the blinding white air as a cover. There is so much to do, so much to plan for, so much to oversee—yet I am not in the least burdened by the prospect of so much work. I thrive in it, I delight at the thought, and it is as if I have waited all my life to get to this moment in time. Nothing and no one will stand in my way now. This is my destiny, the one that I have waited all my life to fulfil.

I travel the length and breadth of Shrinagara—as I used to do before—visiting families, holding processions, addressing the crowds at temples and other congregation areas. I project myself as their mother, someone who cares deeply for their wellbeing and happiness. I distribute money from the treasury to those in dire need and simultaneously undertake a series of public welfare measures. I provide employment at the palace and in the provinces to those who are in need and deserving. I give instructions that any subject with a grievance should not be denied an audience with me, that all genuine complaints merit immediate redressing.

I am everywhere, all over my realm, all at once. And slowly, my people start to revere me as before. They hail

151

me, offer prayers for my health, shout out blessings on the streets, acknowledge me as their ruler. The outrage subsides, the mistrust vanishes—and I have quelled them as surely as if I have personally convinced each person of their falseness. I know that the loyalty of my subjects is fickle, that they might rise against me as easily as they support me today. Yet for now, all is well.

I arrive, unannounced, at the Diddasvamin temple to offer prayers of gratitude. It is a fortnight since I crowned myself but my duties have kept me from coming here so far. The few worshippers who are there at this early hour prostrate themselves before me. It amuses me to note that they are more reverential towards me than to the deity of Vishnu enshrined within, who merits only a perfunctory obeisance today. I savour the moment and their adoration.

Later, I linger by the stone parapet that encircles the temple. The palace looms in the distance, its spire wrapped in white, its bulk deceptively halved in the snow-laden air. A column of orange appears near it, all at once, alternately appearing and fading before my eyes like a mirage. I peer, trying hard to identify it, but the gusts of snow veil my view, frustrating my aim and making me turn away sharply to shield my face.

'Let us go back,' I call to Valga and my guards, my mind filled with a sudden disquiet. For a moment, I wish I had brought Tunga with me today but I had set out with just her and these two men. I try to shake off the worry that has me in its grip but it settles in my mind, squat and forbidding.

As we near the palace, the heavy air lifts to show me line upon line of saffron-clad men before the gates, many hundreds in number, their faces set and grim.

A memory tugs at me, something indistinctly remembered, and then the fog lifts and I know what I am looking at. This is a *prayopavesha*, a rigorous fast adopted by the brahmanas of the kingdom to create chaos, to cause disturbances that shake the foundations of the throne. This is the format they adopt—lining up in rows outside the palace and refusing to leave till they are satisfied.

I am not afraid of their curses for I do not believe that a mortal can mimic a god. But I am scared of the power of this formidable group, of their anger and the havoc they can wreak. As I step out of the carriage, mustering my courage, I see the ones nearest to me smile. The smiles are smug, contemptuous, demeaning. In their minds, they have already won for how can a feeble woman such as me stand up to them or pose any more than the most pitiful resistance? They are clearly unafraid of me—their expressions and stances tell me so.

Anger wells in me, crushing my fear and replacing it with courage. I will show them what a woman's fury is all about. I will show them who their ruler is.

I stand before them, bold and straight, my eyes roving coldly over their lines.

'Who is your leader?' I call.

There is no answer, no movement in response.

'Is he a coward?' I taunt. Beside me, I can hear Valga's stifled gasp of fear.

The lines part and I see someone coming towards me through the rows of tightly-packed men. I recognise him as soon as he moves forward but I do not let my face betray this. He is two paces away when I speak, halting him in his tracks.

'Is *this* all that you are capable of, cousin?' I ask dismissively.

Vigraharaja bridles with rage, unable to frame a coherent reply. This is the effect that I desired. I have already drawn ahead of him in this battle.

VALGA

When I see him after all these years, it is a shock but I pull my features into blankness because I take my cue from her. I marvel at her stance—poised and serene and confident—in this sea of hostile faces.

'Let me go to my palace,' she demands. 'There is no honour in you if you detain a woman in this cowardly manner. In return, I will consider your grievances and do what I can about them.'

Vigraharaja is livid but they let us go.

He stretches his hand toward her in fury, his fingers curved like claws as if he wants to wrap them around her neck. I pull her back and move forward, my strong frame a bulwark between her and him. His eyes blaze with recognition, with the remembrance of our enmity.

The two guards forge a way through the saffron path and we walk calmly towards the palace gate. It swings open, a frightened guard peering through its chinks, and slams shut as soon as we are through. Knowing that they cannot see her now, Didda limps hurriedly towards the palace, her steps quicker than ever before, leaving fast-disappearing footprints in the snow. I follow her, reaching out to steady her when she stumbles, my breath rasping in my throat. I am sweating despite the cold and my heart is pounding with panic.

Tunga comes racing towards her, followed by the palace guards. His face is flushed with fever or fear—I am not sure which it is.

'Secure all the gates!' she cries. 'They must not get through.'

Sharp orders fill the air, along with the tangible smell of panic. I can taste it on my lips, feel it on my skin. Soldiers run past us, clattering out of the doorway into the courtyard. The attendants swarm around us, the maids almost hysterical with terror.

It takes a while for some sort of calm to be restored. By then, we know what they want: the rule of a man— Vigraharaja—rather than that of a woman.

Tunga is ordered to hide in the innermost recesses of the palace, a dark dingy place that has never seen the sunlight and crawls with hideous insects, a place that is sometimes used to incarcerate prisoners. He argues with her but she stands firm.

'If they storm the palace, they will look for you before anybody else,' she says, 'and I cannot risk that.'

'Who will defend you if they do?' He is mutinous, outraged.

'My guards will. Do this for me, Tunga. I cannot bear to lose you now.'

His face softens, relents. Taking her hand gently, he entreats her: 'Take care of yourself. Promise me you will not do anything foolhardy.'

She nods and smiles. Once he is gone, she is everywhere at once—assembling the officers, organising a quick inventory of the treasury, sending spies out into the city to muster support and appraise the situation.

And then, she breaks the rebellion.

She summons the brahmanas, who stand before her, a scowling, unpleasant bunch of men, shivering and discomfited, tugging their saffron robes more closely around their shoulders.

She does not waste time in niceties, but comes straight to the point. A heavy box lies before her, full to the brim with coins from the treasury.

'Name your price,' she says.

And they do.

When none but Vigraha and his few followers are left, Didda orders him to be captured and brought before her. We hear him arguing furiously with his captors as they drag him into the palace; he is a fool not to have anticipated this.

She slaps him—a single, resounding blow to the face that makes him reel back against the guards. An angry red mark blooms on his cheek.

'I should kill you,' she says harshly, 'for taking my parents' lives—but I will give you a far worse fate than that. I will send word to all the kingdoms nearby that you are a rebel, an ingrate, a dangerous man, that they should not let you into their realms. You will get no support, no food, no shelter. And on the day you die, starving and alone, remember the deeds that brought you to this.'

'I will survive!' he screams. 'I will find a way to ...'

'You fool!' Her voice is colder than the snow outside. 'You'll be lucky to last a single day.' She turns to the guards. 'Throw him out of the city.'

His wails echo in the air long after he has left. It is unlikely that he will survive for much longer in this freezing, relentless winter with no one to help him, with nothing to aid his survival—but he has brought this upon himself. If she had executed him on the spot, she would have been more merciful.

Tunga returns to the light, full of vengeance towards those who would question his position. He is as ruthless as Didda in his campaign to destroy the opposition. His inquiries are meticulous and thorough; so are the reports of his spies. Sulakkana, Rakka's son, who is later discovered to have spearheaded the rebellion and urged the brahmanas to revolt, is interrogated and killed. His body, that bears the marks of torture, is thrown into the Vitasta, and later dragged out and thrown on the garbage heaps for the dogs to feast upon.

There are several others who have soiled their hands. They are executed in public, their families forced to look on. The brahmanas who had taken the royal bribes, and whose names had been painstakingly noted by one of the court scribes at the time, are rounded up by Tunga's guards and thrown into prison. The coins are returned, intact, to the royal coffers—there has been no time to spend them.

Revenge is complete; the reprisals are over. Didda issues a proclamation to the people of her realm—whoever challenges her senior officers are indirectly challenging her, and this will be construed as treason and dealt with accordingly. Peace descends one more on the beleaguered land, this time to stay. Didda resumes her processions, her visits to the people, and the street corners are filled with crowds chanting her praises, looking at her with genuine warmth.

Few rulers have been like this—able to surmount one obstacle after another and hold sway all through. And she is a cripple at that! This is why she commands their respect; this is why they hail her rule. And this is how she fulfils her destiny—for generations to come will remember her as the queen who established her rule on this land so effectively that none dared oppose her at the end.

This is how her memory will be evoked.

THE FUTURE OF A KINGDOM

DIDDA

I run my hands through the coins. They are newly minted, firm to the touch yet with a deceptively liquid look to the markings that bear my name, my insignia. This is the latest batch to be produced but the thrill that courses through me is the same as when I beheld the first. I order the officer to put them away and then I walk out of the palace into the sunshine.

My steps are slow and cautious, my body heavy with age and fatigue and recurrent disease. They say I am still beautiful but the grey strands among my hair are plentiful and the wrinkles on my face run across it like a spider's web. Yet from within, my senses are intact, my reactions as sharp as they always were, my decisions as astute.

I walk towards the gardens that are heavy with fruit and vibrant with life. A riot of colours greets me and the hem of my silk robe is stained green by the grass. Heavy perfumes linger in the air and follow me as I walk among the flowers. Purple crocuses nod their heads in unison and quiver in the slight breeze that springs up as if to greet me. Soon their saffron spice will be extracted and used to flavour the rice dishes and sweetmeats prepared in the royal kitchens.

I will never tire of the beauty of this land, its paradisiacal loveliness—although I have learnt that it cloaks the cruelty and ruthlessness of its people. As I drink in the fragrances and sights of summer, I know that winter is close on its heels, that the land will lie shrouded in white before too long.

I hear his footsteps rustling through the long grass towards me and I smile. He has taught me over the years that I am capable of real affection, of warmth, even of love. He has blunted my harshness, softened my severity, and I am now at peace with myself. He has helped to make me the unquestioned power in this land and maintain myself on the throne. He has helped me to fulfil my destiny.

'A flower among the flowers,' he laughs.

I smile at the compliment but my mood quickly turns sombre. 'What happens after me?' I ask.

He stares at me, his green eyes flashing with indignation.

A leaf flutters past me to the ground, and I catch it in my hands and crush it between my fingers. A faint smell of apple clings to my skin. I hold the withered fragments out to him. 'Look, it doesn't exist any more.'

'So?' He knows exactly what I am talking about but he chooses to feign ignorance.

'I won't live forever, Tunga. My next illness could be my last. I need to plan for the kingdom, for what lies ahead.'

'There is time for that yet,' he says impatiently but his eyes are full of dread. I know he cannot think of a life without me.

'I need to appoint a successor,' I say briskly. 'Someone whom I can train now to take over after me.'

'Who will you choose?' he asks curiously. I am relieved somewhere in a part of my mind. He does not desire the throne; he does not hunger for power. I have always known this but each reiteration reinforces my faith and I wish I could throw this in the face of his detractors—and there are still so many of them.

'One of my nephews,' I explain, 'and not just Udayaraja's children. I will include my distant cousins and other relatives in this. Let their children also stand a fair chance.'

He nods. I know that he understands my motive in this wide selection. If my successor is chosen from among several contenders, no one can raise accusations of partiality.

'Will you include the girls?'

'No.' I have considered this. Our line is plentiful in sons, not in daughters. There is only one girl from the family of a remote relative beyond Gandhara who has been reared in seclusion. She will have no knowledge of the world, of its dangers and trials. The one who succeeds me to the throne of Kashmira must be aware, must have knowledge of the world around him, must understand the nature of people. So I have no option but to choose from among the males.

'What about King Kshemagupta's line?' The question is tentative, as if he fears to annoy me by voicing it.

I am very clear on this point. The throne of Kashmira will go to my natal line, not to that of my late husband's. I have forged my path and come all this way on my own despite the opposition of his line and so, I will now bequeath the throne to mine.

There is no time to waste. All of a sudden, I feel as if the days are running out and that death stalks me at every corner.

I send emissaries to Udayaraja along with many gifts for his family, bidding him to send his three sons to me. I have never gone back to Lohara nor has he been able to spare the time to visit me, yet our ties of affection have never frayed or weakened. He has sent me news of every single occurrence in his kingdom—be it the birth of his sons or treaties concluded with border states. If I am truthful to myself, I know that he holds a bigger place in my heart than anybody else in this world, even Tunga or Valga or, in fact, my dead son, Abhimanyu. Strange is this bond of love that does not even require physical proximity to grow!

Messengers are sent to my other relatives as well, anyone who has a grown son to stake his claim for my throne. I receive prompt, eager responses, which makes me laugh at the extent of their greed. In all these years, none of them have bothered about me but now it seems as if I have unleashed a deluge of blessings, good wishes and concern. This is such stark irony!

I have shared the details of my plan with the court and the people at large. There is a huge advantage in having a public contest. Let the people see for themselves the virtues of their future king. Let them acknowledge that this is a fair and unbiased selection. Let them understand that I will choose an able successor.

I know that Tunga has misgivings about what I propose to do. He fears I will select someone unworthy, thereby dragging the kingdom back in time and progress.

I will show him and the others. I will select the best, the worthiest, the brightest among the candidates—and he will follow in my stead.

As my nephews start coming in, I greet them with warmth but scan them with severity. They are of differing ages; the youngest is eight, the oldest seventeen. They are wary of each other, as children will be at first, but then someone organises a game in the courtyard and it is as if they have known each other for ever. The palace rings with childish voices, with their sounds and screams, and my mind jolts back for a second to the past. I can hear Abhimanyu's infant chuckles, his lisping tones as a baby. I can even hear my grandsons' voices float in the air.

I am suddenly nauseous with blinding regret and Valga grasps my hand.

'You are shaking,' she notes, concerned. 'Do you feel well?'

I nod, gently lifting her fingers off mine. There is a reason why the past should remain in the past. It is fruitless to piece it apart in the present. It is but a momentary weakening and I am back to my usual toughness.

As the evening progresses, I watch one boy in particular. Udayaraja's oldest son, Sangramaraja. He is sixteen and looks so like his father that I find myself warming to him at once. A fine, strapping youth, he keeps himself slightly aloof from the rest of the noisy throng. He is perhaps a loner, I reflect.

The following morning, I gather the boys in the public square of the palace. Most have not slept well—their eyes are red and strained, their stance tired. Their families' ambitions ride on them, after all, and this is a huge burden to carry. Their eyes flick nervously to the onlookers who have gathered to watch the selection of their next king and whose loud voices now appraise them.

The guards stationed at each corner of the square look on, impassive. They will intervene if the crowds turn aggressive but I do not think this eventuality will arise. The people's trust in me is implicit; they will not question my decision.

I beckon the boys closer. 'Pay attention,' I command and they all lean forward, the smaller ones elbowing the others so as to be able to see.

I glance around to be sure that everyone is listening and then I continue: 'I will throw before you all a heap of apples. How many can each of you get hold of?'

The question hangs in the air like a challenge. A servant moves to the centre of the square and upends a sack. Rosy apples tumble out in a bouncing heap. I nod to the boys, the signal for them to start, and then retreat to a corner to watch them.

One of them, the tallest and heaviest, strides forward, pushing the others out of his way roughly, and begins to gather the apples. As many as he grasps fall away but he continues, undeterred. Another boy is scrambling around on his hands and knees, desperately gathering the fruit in his hands. Some others are looking around quickly, trying to estimate the number of apples nearest them.

A small knot of boys, meanwhile, is gathered around Sangramaraja and he is talking to them earnestly, his hands gesturing in the air. What is he saying? Why isn't he gathering apples? Who is to win this contest?

VALGA

I am nearest to the group of boys around Sangramaraja, and I see some of them flush angrily and shout out insults. For a moment, I think they are targeting him but they turn away and fall on the other boys who are on their knees, gathering apples. I look with astonishment at Sangramaraja who is standing calmly, arms folded across his chest, his lips curving in a slight smile. He doesn't seem interested in the apples or the contest. Doesn't he even want to try?

As I look on, he beckons to a few others and begins talking to them again. Soon they turn away from him, their faces full of fury, and fall on the others, tearing their clothes, kicking and biting them. Apples roll around the square, dusty and discarded.

I watch the boys writhe in a twisting, screaming heap, limbs flailing and lashing out, pounding away at each other, hurling the choicest of insults—and then I watch Sangramaraja walk calmly away from them and start to pick up the apples. He does this unhurriedly, as if he is in an orchard with all the time in the world to select the choicest fruit. He makes a fold in his tunic to contain the apples and within minutes, he has gathered almost all of them. The boys are still fighting furiously with each other as he makes his way towards Didda with his gatherings.

At a gesture from her, a servant walks into the breach, clapping his hands. 'The time is up,' he bellows into the chaos. 'The contest is over.'

It takes some time for the boys to disentangle themselves, for order to be restored—and then there is a startled silence. They look at Sangramaraja and his apples, bitter realisation dawning on their faces. Later, we learn that he has made them fight with each other while keeping himself away from the fray. He is already a master strategist.

Didda's face is transformed by joy and I know with certainty that this is what she has wanted all along. She kept the contest fair and open but her heart's desire was to make Sangramaraja her heir. What could be better, after all, than to have the son of her beloved brother succeed her to the throne?

168

She holds Sangramaraja's hand aloft to proclaim him the winner.

'He is your next ruler,' she cries to the assembled populace. 'You have seen him win the deciding contest.'

Before Sangramaraja takes up permanent residence in Shrinagara, he requests leave to return to Lohara and share his happiness with his parents. It is readily granted. Sangramaraja is to bear gifts and loving missives for his parents from her. He is to return in a fortnight and then there will be a grand ceremony to formally proclaim him as Didda's heir. She hopes that Udayaraja and his wife will return with their son to attend the ceremony.

The night before his departure, Didda summons him and Tunga to her in her private audience chamber, dismissing all her other attendants except for me.

'There is one last thing you must do for me before you go,' she tells him. Then she turns to Tunga. 'And you, too.'

The prince looks expectant; Tunga, baffled. 'What is it?' he asks quickly. 'Has something happened?'

'Not yet,' she responds, 'but I must make sure it doesn't happen.'

She looks from one to the other. 'I want you to take a sacred oath before me, both of you, and it is this: that you will not harm each other after I am gone, that you will support each other in the governance of this kingdom. You, Sangramaraja, will regard Tunga as your mentor and advisor. And you, Tunga, will protect him as you have protected me. Now swear to this.'

'Do you doubt my intentions?' Tunga sounds bitter.

She shakes her head vehemently. 'How can you say that?' she asks softly. 'You are my greatest support and always have been. If you had wanted the throne, you could have seized it from me many times over.' She looks at them earnestly. 'I am doing this to protect both of you. I trust you but not those around you—and there is no dearth of mischief-makers who will try to cause a rift between you. This is what I am trying to prevent. Do you understand?'

They nod and, in a matter of a few minutes, the deed is done. They will now be each other's greatest strength for the oath they have taken is sacred and binding. Relief washes over Didda's face. Her greatest fear has now been averted.

The securing of the future and the prospect of seeing her beloved brother again has lent a brightness to her face. She looks almost as she did in earlier years—luminous, vibrant, expectant, humming with vivacity.

But this does not deceive those of us who are close to her. I see Tunga glance at her with acute concern several times and I, of course, am alert and watchful, standing behind her as always to support her with my strength. I note the deep pallor on her face, her eyes that are heavy with exhaustion. There is no disguising the truth. She is nearing her end. She knows it; I know it, too.

It is an autumn evening and the shadows cloak Sangramaraja's convoy as it advances down the palace courtyard. Tunga and his men will escort it as far as the outskirts of the city. We stand and watch the weaving line of men until we can't tell them apart from the darkness and then she guides me to the garden. The breeze is swift and cold, and dry leaves spin down from the trees that surround us, carpeting our footsteps and rustling under our weight. It is silent expect for the occasional cries of roosting birds and we can hear the Vitasta's waves lapping lazily against each other. Its waters will be very cold now, I think, and shiver at the thought.

'You're trembling. Are you ill?' she asks and I shake my head. My strength has not waned in old age; it has remained the one constant in my life. My hair is grey like hers, my face is wrinkled but my body is still as strong as an ox.

We do not speak but the silence between us is comfortable. We have known each other for so long that words are often unnecessary, a mere burden that we can dispense with. I think of Naravahana, the third part of us, and I am not surprised when she asks, 'Are you thinking of our friend?'

I nod and she grasps my hand, holding it tightly. 'He is in my mind as well. My work is done; everything is settled. What would he say to that? Do you think he knows?' Her voice is heavy as if with tears but her eyes are dry.

'He does.' I curl my fingers against hers. 'He knows that you have fulfilled your destiny.'

'Did I achieve greatness? Just like they said I would?' Her voice is uncertain and I am now suddenly so full of conflicting emotions that I catch my breath. I have known her for almost as long as I have lived——as a girl filled with uncertainty, poised on the brink of her ambition; a woman who came into her own and followed a path littered with harsh decisions; a queen, now on the edge of death, who has led a kingdom for five decades and assured its future so emphatically.

I have followed her wherever she went, stood by her side at every step she took, shared my strength with her when she needed it, been her shadow through all her days. There is no more bitterness, no remorse, no sorrow. My doubts have been quelled by love, my anger with affection.

When I rescued her from Vigraharaja in our girlhood, I did not know where that single act would lead me; I did not foresee that it would bring about this long journey of friendship, of togetherness. Yet now I know, as surely as if I have written my own fate, that I will not live without her, that I will follow her as I have always done, even into the shadows. This thought, this certainty, makes me smile and my heart lifts, all at once, like a bird.

'Why are you silent, Valga? Do you think I achieved greatness?'

'Yes, you have.' My voice rings with firmness, with conviction. 'And those who come after us will know you for this. Your name will be handed down from generation to generation in Kashmira as one to be respected and cherished. If this isn't greatness, then what is?'

She tips her head back and looks up at the night sky. Its blackness is terrifying, yet its star-studded immensity is like a protective shield over the land—a blend, as it were, of malevolence and kindness, of evil and good.

And she smiles.

HISTORICAL NOTE

Didda ruled Kashmir from CE 980/1-1003, representing female power at its vibrant peak in the early medieval period in Indian history. Unfortunately, though, she is a victim of the gender bias that exists in the writing of history. Although she was a masterful ruler who ensured an unprecedented era of peace and prosperity in Kashmir, her rule and contributions have been invisibilised or trivialized in accounts of this period. I have remained faithful to the facts provided by the original sources in the rendition of her story.

The *Rajatarangini* by Kalhana, a Sanskrit text that provides an account of the rulers of Kashmir from the earliest times to the poet's own (CE 1149/50), is the most important source for Didda's history. Didda's influence on her husband, Kshemagupta (CE 950-58) is proved by his coins that rarely bear his name alone but instead that of *di-kshemagupta de(va)*, a conjunction of both their names—and a highly unusual procedure. This corroborates Kalhana's assertion that the king's popular nickname was *diddakshema*.

Didda's influence over Kashmir spanned around fifty years. The text directly implicates her in the deaths of her grandsons, Nandigupta (CE 972-73), Tribhuvana (CE 973-75; also known as Tribhuvanagupta on his rare coins) and Bhimagupta (CE 975-980/1). That she was responsible for the death of her son, Abhimanyu (CE 958-72), is also hinted at.

Didda later issued coins in her capacity as ruler—itself a fairly rare occurrence in early medieval history—that refer to her by masculine epithets (*sri didda deva*). The epigraphic evidence for Didda's reign consists of the Buddhist image inscription of year 65 (CE 989) of her reign and the Srinagar inscription of year 68 (CE 992). The first refers to her by the masculine appellation *deva* while the second uses the feminine term *rajni*.

Not much evidence remains of the intense building activity that Didda indulged in after the death of her son, Abhimanyu. Aurel Stein, on whose translation of the *Rajatarangini* I have relied, notes that her Abhimanyusvamin temple and town of Abhimanyupura cannot be traced, nor the Diddasvamin temple or Diddapura town. However, the matha that she built for the residence of people from Madhyadesha and Lata, among others, can be identified with the Diddamatha that has left its name to the Didmar quarter of Srinagar.

Likewise, the town of Kankanapura that she built in Kshemagupta's memory can be traced to Kangan, a village on the banks of the Indus. Varahakshetra, the place of Kshemagupta's death and where he had founded the Srikanthamatha and Kshemamatha, can be identified with the site and vicinity of Varahamula, the present Baramula. Stein also identifies Bhattarakamatha, where Abhimanyu once sought refuge, as surviving in the Bradmar quarter of Srinagar.

The memory of Didda does not seem to have been confined to the physical landscape, however. Stein notes that at the time of his research, it was apparently customary among Kashmir brahmana families to call the eldest woman of the household by the title 'Didd' in respectful recollection of 'the great queen'.

The *Rajatarangini* refers to Didda as lame, limping, or crippled in the legs. There is no explanation for or description of this disability, however. Likewise, the *luta* disease that Kshemagupta died of remains unclear. All that is known is that it was sudden and fatal in nature, and was characterized by eruptions on the body that resembled split lentils. No known cure existed for it at the time.

Regarding Naravahana, much of his early life is my fabrication. He appears in the *Rajatarangini* only after

Didda's arrival in Kashmir and remains steadfastly loyal to her throughout his life. However, the unusual closeness and warmth between them leads me to speculate that they knew each other for much longer than otherwise indicated—and hence, my detailing of their friendship might be entirely plausible. That he committed suicide due to his inability to handle Didda's sudden frostiness is historical fact.

Valga, the other pillar of this story, is the subject of a single verse in the *Rajatarangini* that refers to her as a 'porter-woman' who used to carry the lame Didda at games which required running and who caused the Valgamatha to be built. My decision to rescue her from obscurity and invest her with importance in Didda's scheme of things was prompted by the consideration that she would have been by the latter's side at all times, perhaps as a silent observer but, nevertheless, privy to Didda's moods and decisions. She was, thus, the perfect voice to provide an alternative angle to Didda's story. It is also entirely plausible that she was a long-standing companion who accompanied Didda to Kashmir.

I have undertaken some license while dealing with Vigraharaja's story. He was, in fact, Didda's nephew, the son of a brother who remains unnamed. Vigraha rebelled against Didda twice—once when he was brought to Kashmir by disaffected ministers to head a rebellion to oust Tunga and again, when he induced the brahmanas to embark upon a fast to cause chaos in the kingdom. In both cases, Didda bought off the protesters with bribes. Vigraha is supposed to have made another attempt on Kashmir after the death of Sangramaraja in CE 1028 when he was defeated and slain. In the interests of the narrative, I have combined all these rebellions into one and brought forward the time of his death.

Didda's decision to bequeath the throne of Kashmir to her natal family of Lohara was a momentous one with far-reaching repercussions. On her death in CE 1003, the throne passed in undisputed succession to Lohara and descendants of the latter held sway in Kashmir even beyond the time of the *Rajatarangini*'s completion. It is interesting to note that both Tunga and Sangramaraja held, for a while, to the vow that Didda, in her political sagacity, had made them observe, until mutual enmities drove them apart.

Didda's maternal grandfather, King Bhima Shahi, who is also known through his coins and inscriptions, is identical with King Bhima whom Alberuni mentions in his list of the Hindu Shahiyas of Kabul as the successor of Kamalu. This dynasty ruled the Kabul valley and Gandhara prior to the conquest of Mahmud of Ghazni. Udabhanda/Udabhandapura was the name of the ancient capital of Gandhara and is referred to by Alberuni as Waihand. Its position is apparently marked by the village of Und on the banks of the Indus. Stein identified Bhima Shahi's shrine of Bhimakeshava with an ancient temple found at Bumzu, a mile to the north of the sacred springs at Martanda. It was subsequently converted into a mosque and became known as the resting-place of a Muslim saint, Baba Bamdin Sahib, thus becoming a popular pilgrimage place for the Muslims of the valley.

Kashmira (modern Kashmir) at the time of this story was confined to the valley of the Jhelum (Vitasta) and to the inner slopes of the ring of mountains that surround it. The Chinese pilgrim, Yuan Chwang, who visited the capital city of Kashmira in about CE 631, found it already in the position of the present Srinagar. He describes it as situated along the bank of a great river, the Vitasta. Lohara, Didda's maternal home, refers to the territory comprising the mountain districts immediately adjoining Kashmir to the south-west. It pertains to the modern Lohrin valley which is now included in the Poonch district.

Didda formed part of my doctoral research on women in early medieval north India. More information can be found in my book, *Invisible Women, Visible Histories: Gender, Society and Polity in North India (Seventh to Twelfth Century AD)* (Manohar: 2009).

Dr Devika Rangachari is an award-winning children's writer who is also pursuing her post-doctoral research in Indian history from the University of Delhi.

Devika is extremely fond of historical fiction and is usually wandering somewhere in the past. She reads more than she writes until friendly-yet-stern editors feed her copious quantities of chocolate and tell her to get started. At this point, her nephew and niece chivvy her into being focused—the one by counting aloud the number of words and the other, by pouncing on stray grammatical errors. Once the book is done, Devika floats gently back into the world of history.